# SCRITCH SCRATCH

## THE LEGEND OF TEKETEKE

E. L. JULIAN

Scritch Scratch: The Legend of Teketeke (Paperback Edition, 2024)
ISBN Paperback: 978-1-0670150-4-6
ISBN Epub: 978-1-0670150-1-5
ISBN Audiobook: 978-1-0670150-3-9

Cover design and interior formatting by: E. L. Julian
Editing and proofreading by: Sharron McKenzie
Chapter head image, character art and author image illustrated by: E. L. Julian

For my mentor, Ronnie,
without whom this book would not exist as it is today.

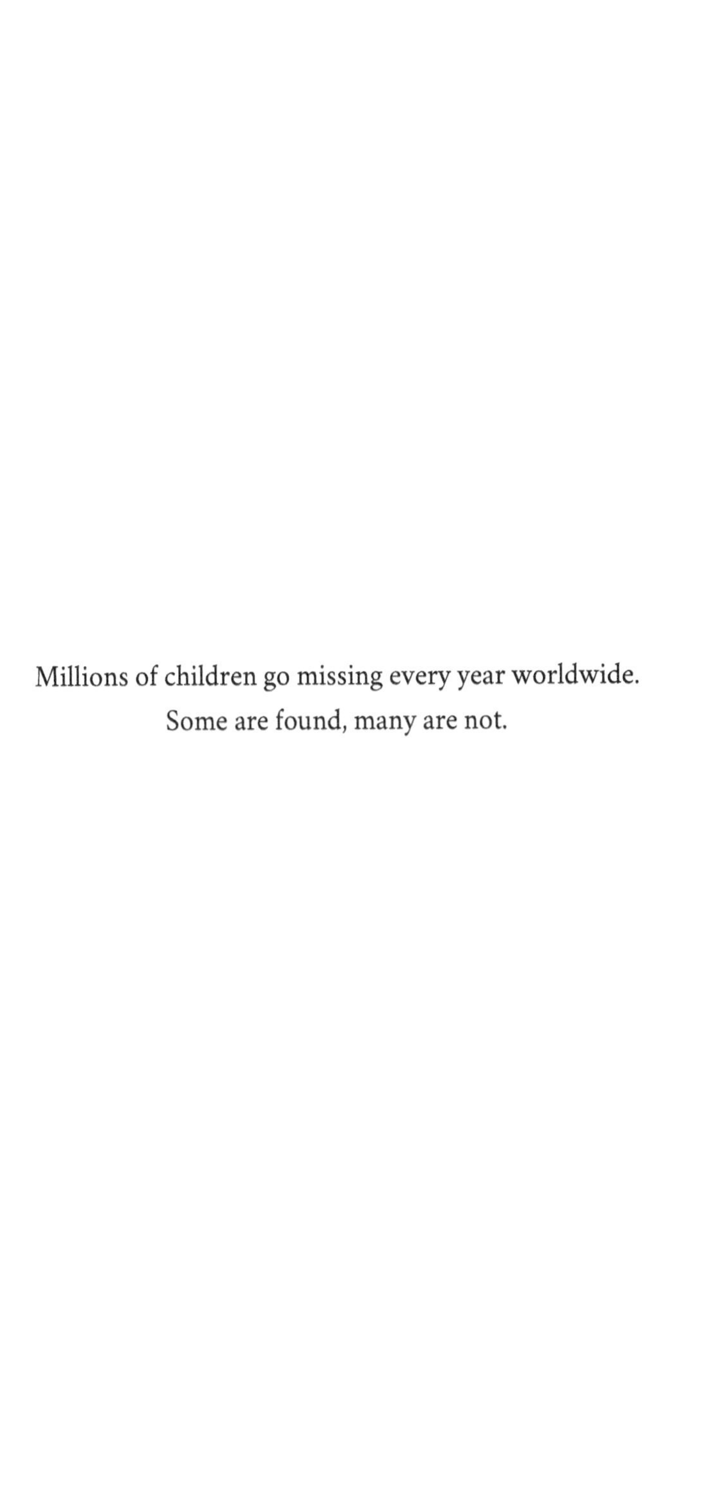

Millions of children go missing every year worldwide.
Some are found, many are not.

# Teketeke

## The Legend

Most people have been afraid of the dark at some time or another. I mean, what's not to be afraid of?

Many of us rely on sight for 90% of our 'data' on what's going on around us. But in the dark, we lose that. We have to rely on sound, touch, and smell to navigate our surroundings, which is mildly terrifying for those who are not used to doing so. That is why I think *Teketeke* is such a scary urban legend.

Japan has a wide variety of urban legends, many of which focus on vengeful spirits known as *onryo*. *Teketeke* is one such legend. There are a few variations, but the general story goes that *Teketeke* is the spirit of a girl who fell onto train tracks just as the train was arriving and was cut clean in half. Her spirit tends to haunt urban areas, usually at night.

*Teketeke*, in Japanese, roughly translates to *scritch scratch* in English, but is literally 'the onomatopoeia of a body dragging along the floor.' Very specific, I know. Because she was cut in half, *Teketeke* must drag herself along the ground using her hands or elbows; the sound she makes is how she came to be known as *Teketeke*.

According to legend, if you were ever to cross her path, she would chase you down at an alarming speed and slice you in half with her scythe.

So, if you ever hear the *scritch scratching* of a body dragging across the ground at night, in the darkness… run.

# Editor's Note

Looking back now, as an author, learning Japanese in New Zealand is quite unique compared to the UK and the US. I never thought anything odd about it at the time, but our textbooks used an interesting combination of British English and American English.

For example, we learned that 大学 (*daigaku*) was to be translated as 'university,' yet 小学校 (*shogakkou*) was 'elementary school.' Very odd, considering we use the British 'primary school' and 'intermediate' (instead of 'junior high school') here in New Zealand.

But I never questioned this, and thus, this 'Combination English' has become my natural go-to when translating from Japanese to English.

In saying that, while researching this book, I noticed that Google maps does the same thing: the names of Japanese tertiary education providers show up as '—University,' rather than 'College,' while 'middle schools' are called 'JHS' (Junior High School).

While the editor in me wants to change everything to strictly either UK or US spelling, I feel that this combination is a representation of my nine years of Japanese education under the New Zealand curriculum. I suppose it can't be too wrong if it shows as such on maps, right?

So I decided to keep the translations as they are.

Now, if you need me, I'll be in my bunker, hiding from my editor. (I knew I should have hidden all the knives until after the release date...)

# SCRITCH SCRATCH

Saitama, Japan 2020

"URGH, THIS IS such a drag…" Officer Kawada groaned, warming his fingers on his hot takeaway cup.

"You've been complaining for the last hour." Officer Honda clicked his teeth. "Orders are orders. Now keep your mouth shut and your eyes open."

Officer Yuuki Honda was your typical yes-man and had excelled at the academy. He was gunning for top brass one day; Commissioner General, if he had his way.

*Needs to pull that stick out of his ass*, Kawada thought, the fidgety tapping of his standard-issue shoes hardly making a ripple in the pool of noise. His gaze wandered lazily over the hordes of people coming and going through the main entrance of Ōmiya Station. When he was young, he used to think train stations were like the 'Anywhere Door' from *Doraemon*—a magical portal capable of transporting thousands of people all over Japan. Through his adult eyes, it appeared painfully mundane—normal people on normal commutes. "How can we keep an eye out if we don't even know what we're looking for? 'Anyone suspicious' doesn't really narrow it down."

"Anyone with unreasonably over-sized bags, children travelling alone, lone middle-aged men looking nervous—use your imagination," Officer Honda replied, arms crossed.

Kawada sighed as he smoothed his hair back; the summer's humidity was wreaking its usual havoc. "Other prefectures don't have extra patrols. What's so special about here?"

"I've heard rumours, but none that hold water. It's what we've been told to do, that's all that matters. You need to know how to follow orders if you want to make a career of this." Most of their conversations were ten percent speaking and ninety percent awkward silences.

A mother with her young daughter stole a glance at them when they walked past. *She must think there's some kind of criminal on the loose or something,* Kawada thought, knowing their presence was probably scaring more people than it was comforting. Especially with Officer Honda looking like a drill sergeant. All he needed was an assault rifle and S.W.A.T vest and the look would be complete.

"We can't watch out for trouble if we die of boredom first. You're from Saitama, right?" Kawada asked. He was desperate for anything to take his mind off the residual hum of the swarm. It was like being inside a beehive after someone shook it a few times.

"Yes, why?"

"You must have some stories. What did you do when you were a kid? Anything interesting?" Kawada tried to picture Officer Honda as a normal, easy-going kid.

"Can't be much different from growing up in... where are you from again? Osaka? Anyway, it's hard to think of something on the spot like that," Officer Honda replied, his eyes darting from person to person as he scanned the masses. "Ah, there is one thing—scared me to death when I was in middle school."

"This sounds promising."

"Me and a couple of friends were just leaving school, later than usual since we got caught up playing baseball, when I noticed a window on the fourth floor of the main building was open. It was hard to miss with the curtains being pulled out, waving in the wind. That's when my friend first told me about *Teketeke*."

"Never heard of it." Kawada noticed a group of high school kids heading towards the West Exit. One of them carried a large sports bag, big enough to fit a small child. The boy wore a cap and a baseball glove, so Kawada didn't bother searching his bag.

"It's an urban legend, especially around Saitama. A boy leaves school late, after dark, when he sees a girl through an open window on the second floor, leaning with her elbows on the windowsill."

"A girl scared you shitless?" Kawada said, drinking down the last of his coffee and tossing it into the recycling bin next to them. "I'm not surprised—they're all pretty fucking scary."

"Very funny. The fact that she was inside an all-boys' school after the gates had all been locked didn't help," Officer Honda replied, clicking his teeth again. "A real beauty, too, apparently. But after he called out to her, he found out that she was somewhat... lacking."

"Lacking what?"

"Her lower body."

Kawada scrunched up his nose. "Sounds like a bad joke."

"Maybe now that we're adults, but it was a terrifying story as a kid. The sound she made was even scarier. The boy turned to run, but all he could hear behind him was the sound of her dragging herself along the ground. That's why they call her Teketeke—scritch scratch."

"So, what happened to the kid?" Kawada asked. His eyes trailed after a stunning woman in a long white dress and designer sunhat. Her wavy black hair was slightly frizzy in the humidity, but she was beautiful, nonetheless.

*Maybe I should search her bag.*

"He was found the next morning cut in half, his lower body missing."

"That's disgusting... You talk about it as if it actually happened."

"It did, in a way. The story even made the papers. The

boy did actually go missing, but they didn't find his mutilated corpse. They didn't find him at all. There was a surge of missing children cases back then. But it's just a silly legend—nothing to lose sleep over."

"Is that a fact?" Sergeant Sasaki's deep baritone voice tore them from their conversation. The veteran police officer had not a hair out of place, although the odd wisp of grey affirmed his advancing age. He stared at them, his eyes critical and accusing. Deep, dark circles under his eyes made him look old and haggard. *I wonder how ancient the old goat really is*, Kawada thought.

"Care to tell me why you're standing here talking instead of patrolling the rest of the station? There's more to look at than just this area. The North, South, and East Exits, for example. Did it even cross your minds to check people going on and off the platforms? Not everyone gets off here."

"No, sir. I'm sorry, sir. We were just—" Officer Honda tried to explain, when Sergeant Sasaki cut him off, his voice sharp as a switchblade.

"Take my advice. Don't talk about that story or those missing children cases again. Not at our station, not at any station in Saitama, or I will personally oversee your transfers. Understood?"

"Y-yes sir…" In less than a minute, Officer Honda had lost all colour. His forehead glistened with fresh sweat.

"Good. Now come with me. If you look up 'patrol' in the dictionary, I think you'll find that it says, 'to watch over an area by walking or travelling around it.'" Sergeant Sasaki walked on ahead of them, his head turning left and right.

*Jeez, no need to bite our heads off. It's not like anyone died,* Kawada thought, his lips pursed as they headed towards the entrance to the nearest platform. The stairs were crammed with people. Kawada tried not to accidentally jab anyone with his elbow while he made his way down.

A hard jolt to the side made Kawada cry out. "Hey!"

A man in a navy blue cap and black t-shirt quickened his pace and passed Kawada, pulling his cap further over his face.

*Asshole. Could've at least apologised,* Kawada thought bitterly. Sergeant Sasaki was already ahead of them on the platform, his face strained with concentration as he scanned both sides of the platforms. Kawada followed his lead.

Most of the crowd was condensed to the right side of the platform, bound for Higashi-Ōmiya. Several women (housewives, judging by their clothes), elementary school kids in bright coloured hats, as well as high schoolers glued to their phones. Nothing odd there. Although Kawada wondered how the hell they could navigate the crowded platform without looking up.

He spotted the man in the blue cap crossing from the left platform to the right side; no phone in his hand, but also with his head bowed low. He didn't look up even once.

Kawada snorted. *That explains a lot. No wonder he bumps into people if he doesn't bother to look where he's going.*

Suddenly, Sergeant Sasaki's head snapped to the right before hurrying to the platform bound for Higashi-Ōmiya.

"Is something wrong?" Officer Honda whispered to

Kawada. Kawada shrugged.

"Beats me."

The familiar sound of an ascending xylophone scale followed by a pre-recorded female voice announcing the train's arrival, blasted over the intercom.

まもなく、一番線に東大宮方面行きがまいります。

*The train bound for Higashi-Ōmiya will arrive momentarily at Platform One.*

危ないですから黄色い線までお下がりください。

*Please wait behind the yellow line.*

Kawada's gaze trailed after Sergeant Sasaki, who was making a beeline towards the man in the blue cap.

*What am I missing...?* His eyes darted from person to person, his heart beating hard and fast the longer he took to find that one missing link. He finally fixed on a little girl, only about six years old, waiting behind the yellow line for the train. She'd taken off her bright yellow school hat, making her almost invisible. Sergeant Sasaki was already beside her, crouching down as he spoke.

The man in the blue cap stopped, turned on his heels, and hurried in the opposite direction. Kawada motioned for Officer Honda to follow the man while he made his way over to Sergeant Sasaki. "You two stay here and keep an eye on things while I see this little one home," Sergeant Sasaki said, smiling down at the girl. It was the most human expression Kawada had ever seen him make, almost paternal.

Looking back, Officer Honda shook his head. The man was long gone.

"How did you notice that guy so quickly, sir? I only thought his behaviour was suspicious after following your lead," Kawada whispered so the little girl couldn't overhear.

"You have to notice these things, Kawada. People's lives depend on it." Sergeant Sasaki took the girl's hand and escorted her onto the train. "I'll be back soon. Kawada, you keep watch here. Honda, you patrol the rest of the station. Don't trust anybody." The train doors slid shut, and the train sped off.

"What was that all about?" Officer Honda asked, wiping his forehead with his pocket handkerchief.

"That girl might have been kidnapped if Sergeant Sasaki hadn't been here," Kawada said, staring at the ground, full of self-loathing. He'd thought of this as a shit assignment with no real merit.

But Sergeant Sasaki just proved that what they did or didn't notice could change someone's life forever.

# ASPIRATIONS

Ten Years Earlier

DING DONG! THE sound of the doorbell woke Hisako from a relaxing sleep. "Oh hi, Sayoko," she heard her mother say. Hisako's eyes snapped open.

"Hi, Mrs Nakamura. Is Hisako home? We had plans to study today," she heard Sayoko reply.

*Crap!* Hisako scrambled out of bed and pulled on a white miniskirt and sweater before shoving all her books and some paper into her shoulder bag and racing down the stairs. "Hey Sayoko," she said, out of breath; smoothing her chestnut-coloured hair.

"Hi Hisako. Did you forget about our early morning study session?" Sayoko asked, looking Hisako up and down. "Fabulous hair, by the way."

A fat white Persian cat came waddling over to Sayoko, brushing against her legs and meowing. "Oh, I'm sorry, Mochi, did I forget to say hi to you?" Sayoko said in the baby tone people use when speaking to animals. The heart-shaped tag attached to Mochi's pale blue collar jingled as she gently scratched under his chin and behind his ears.

"Ha-ha. You're so lucky you're a cat person like me, or I'd totally hate you right now." Hisako giggled, picking up Mochi and scratching him affectionately on the head before passing him to her mother.

"Study hard, girls."

The sun was blindingly bright, the heat stifling and humid, and the cherry blossoms were in full bloom as Hisako and Sayoko set off down the familiar path to the library. They both lived in the same neighbourhood opposite Yono Park, so it was only a short walk to the library and the high school.

They'd just started back a few weeks ago, but it was already hectic with the teachers bombarding them with talks about their futures and preparing for college entrance exams.

"Are you any closer to figuring out which university you want to go to?" Hisako asked, covering her eyes with her hand to block out the sun. The little red man on the crossing display changed to green.

Sayoko sighed, pushing her thick, round glasses up her nose. "The problem isn't figuring out which one I want to go to—I've known that for years: Tokyo U Medical School."

Hisako faked a melodramatic, exasperated sigh. "Don't remind me." She chuckled. "I nearly threw up when we had to dissect frogs last year—you were the only one smiling and having a grand old time. How can you stand all that… grossness?"

"It's fascinating, that's how. Besides, my problem isn't stomaching 'grossness.' It's finding a suitable alternative university in case I don't pass the entrance exam. It's strict, especially for women…" Her voice was a potent combination of disappointment and frustration.

"I know… I've got it easy. There are a million places to study childcare. I heard that Tokyo U marks down women's scores on the exams by twenty percent. Did you hear about that?"

"Of course. On top of that, their acceptance rate is only eight percent. Even with the required GPA, I'm already at a disadvantage. Then, if I do get in, I have to be able to keep up with the curriculum."

"I know you can do it. Want some help looking up some other medical schools while we're at the library? Just in case? I already know I'm going to Urawa University, so I've got the time."

"Thanks, that would really help."

Sayoko tucked a long strand of silky black hair behind her ear, a warm smile on her face. Hisako could almost always tell what Sayoko was thinking, even though she had never been much of a talker. But Hisako's mother always said that you could tell what lay in a person's heart based on how they treated animals, and Sayoko had loved Mochi since the first day she came over.

It was then Hisako knew that they'd be best friends.

"Satoru started elementary school the other day, didn't he? How did it go? Has he made any friends yet?" Sayoko asked as she pushed open the doors to Yono Library. It was small compared to other libraries in Saitama, but was the most convenient. Its cold, concrete structure stood out; every other house looked like a mini farm with well-kept plots of produce in back gardens. The smell of roses wafted over from the Rose Garden at Yono Park.

"Yeah, he did. He's loving it so far. He can already write his name in *kanji*, can you believe that? I'm telling you, he's going to be as smart as you one day." Hisako beamed. Sayoko secured a free table (not an easy task, with the first round of entrance exams next January) while Hisako found a free computer.

"Let's look up some alternative schools for you first, then we can move on to English and math," Hisako said, opening a browser. "Do you want universities near Saitama or national?"

"Definitely Saitama."

# BUTTERFLY DREAMER

"I'M HOME," SAYOKO called as she removed her shoes and put them neatly on the shoe rack in the entryway.

"In here, honey," her mother replied. Sayoko threw her bag on the floor and went into the open-plan living, dining, and kitchen area. The room was warm and inviting from the smell of garlic, salt, and frying fish; steam billowed from the rice cooker on the bench as her mother opened the lid and transferred the piping hot rice into a wooden serving bowl.

Sayoko heard the door slam, followed by her father's voice. "I'm home."

"Welcome home, dear. Perfect timing. Dinner's almost ready," Sayoko's mother said. They all took a seat at the dining table and said grace.

"You're home early, Sayoko. How did the studying go?"

Sayoko's father asked, in between mouthfuls. He was still in his navy police uniform but had removed the tailored jacket and loosened his tie.

"Good. Hisako helped me make a list of alternative medical schools. I've narrowed it down to a few near here, as well as Kyoto and Osaka."

"It's good to have alternatives, but you know what I always say…"

"'He who chases two hares gets none,' I know, Dad. I've got my eye on the target, don't you worry."

Sayoko's mother filled Sayoko's rice bowl and passed it to her. "Did any of these universities sound promising? I hope they aren't too far away."

"Dokkyo Medical University in Tochigi sounds like the best one. They have an impressive variety of classes and fields depending on what you want to specialise in. Second would be Saitama Medical University, I suppose." Sayoko ripped the head off her fried fish and sucked out the eyes, savouring the jelly-like texture as they melted in her mouth. "I still want to go into Tokyo-U, Osaka-U, and Kyoto-U to talk to someone about what options they have. I'll have to study my tail off to even have a hope in hell of getting in." Sayoko took a long sip of her miso soup. "I'll pay a visit to all the other universities I found as well. It can't hurt." Sayoko gave her parents a small smile.

"Sounds like you're well prepared." Her father sipped at his chilled beer.

"I've got it all planned out. I can study on the train. So, I might be home late more often than not, between the commuting and the studying. Do you mind?"

"Not at all, dear. Do you need anything for the train fare?" her mother asked.

"Yes, please. That would be great. Although the bullet train to Kyoto and Osaka might be expensive…" Sayoko drank the last of her miso soup, then stacked her bowls before taking them to the kitchen to rinse off.

"Just let me know when you want to go and I'll loan you my bullet train pass," her father said, leaning back into his chair. His eyes were puffier than usual, his face pale and haggard.

"Really? Thanks, Dad." Sayoko put her dishes back in the cupboard and headed towards the stairs. "I'm going to go study some more."

"Don't overwork yourself," her mother said. "Will Hisako be going with you to these universities? I'd feel better about you travelling if you were with someone…"

Sayoko stopped mid-step, already halfway up the stairs. "No. She's already decided to go to Urawa-U. I'll be fine by myself. The stations are always well-policed. Just ask Dad."

Sayoko's father smirked and nodded.

"That's a shame. But I'm sure no matter where you end up going, you two will stay close," her mother continued.

"I hope so," Sayoko replied.

Sayoko closed her bedroom door and opened her math book. It was a necessary evil if she wanted to study medicine.

She began to lose her concentration after only half an hour. Giving up, she threw her glasses onto her desk and leaned back, in a daze.

Various insects in white picture frames hung from almost every wall, along with anatomy posters and the odd brightly coloured anime poster. A compact, portable ant farm sat on one of the lower levels of her bookshelf, accompanied by an insane number of books. Piles of books were even stacked up next to her bed. She had everything, from non-fiction books on entomology, *Grey's Anatomy*, and medical books by Atul Gawande; to Shojo manga and light novels. Hisako had recommended most of the latter. She was the first friend Sayoko had made when she'd moved from Hokkaido.

*Eleven years*, Sayoko sighed, putting her glasses back on and staring out the window. *Can people even stay friends when they live so far apart? It's not like we'll have the time to travel back and forwards every other day.*

She rested her chin on her hands, leaning forward on her desk as her mind wandered.

Little Sayoko sat outside, watching her parents go in and out of their new house, shouting instructions to the movers about where to put all the furniture.

They now lived across the road from a park. Sayoko could see other kids swinging on swings and sliding down slides, screaming with laughter.

"Why don't you go over and play with them?"

Sayoko hadn't heard her mother sneak up behind her. Her mouth puckered into a pout as she ran up and hugged her mother's legs, tugging on her skirt. "Come on, don't be shy. I'm sure they're all very nice. Won't it be nice to make a friend or two before you start school?"

Sayoko squeezed her mother's legs tighter, her whispers muffled. "What if they don't like me?"

"They'll love you. But first you have to actually go over there." Her mother's warm smile gave Sayoko the boost of courage she needed.

She looked both ways before crossing the street, her little heart pounding as she went straight over to the playground.

The entire park smelt of wet grass and fresh roses.

*Wow,* she thought when she passed a water fountain built into the pavement; kids were filling buckets and floating toy boats down the little waterfall. She splashed her hands in the cool water. She wasn't used to the warm weather yet. It was so much colder in Hokkaido, even in the summer.

Trees covered the jungle-gym and playground, so if anyone fell, it would be onto soft grass and dirt. Sayoko stood in front of the playground, scrunching up her pink skirt in her hands as she swayed from side to side, glancing around as if she was lost.

All the other kids already had playmates and none of them saw her standing there, waiting for an invitation. She was about to climb the first step up the ladder to the slide when something caught her eye in the dirt by a nearby tree. Sayoko crept over, crouching down to get a better look.

It was a monarch butterfly.

*Pretty...* Sayoko crawled onto her stomach, supporting herself on her elbows. The butterfly was twitching its wings, trying to fly away; both wings were injured, and the usually vibrant orange had faded to a dull orange-brown.

*It must have gotten wet in the rain this morning.* Sayoko cautiously stroked its velvety wings with her index finger. They felt soft and fragile, like rice paper.

Sayoko kicked her feet as she watched the creature struggle. When an army of ants climbed down the tree trunk and marched towards the struggling butterfly, she squealed and jerked her hand away. She didn't want them climbing all over her, too. As the ants swarmed around the butterfly, she stared in silence, amazed that something so small could lift something so much heavier. She watched them rip the butterfly apart, devouring it slowly, piece by piece. It was the most beautiful thing she had ever seen.

"What'cha looking at?"

Sayoko looked up to find a little girl with short brown hair standing over her. The girl's face changed from a playful smile to shock when she saw the butterfly lying in the dirt, missing its antennae and several legs.

"Uh-oh! Quick, give me your hand," she said, grabbing Sayoko's hand and scooping up the butterfly. "Aaaw. I wonder if we can save it? That's why I hate the rain..." Her eyes went all shiny, like she was about to cry. Tiny holes covered the butterfly's wings where the ants had eaten it. "I'm Hisako. What's your name?"

Sayoko's cheeks flushed, her shyness flooding back. She stared at the dirt. "Um, I'm Sayoko."

"Sayoko. That's a pretty name." Hisako beamed, putting the injured butterfly into the palm of Sayoko's hands. "You tried to help it first, so you can have it, if you want. Put it somewhere safe, okay?"

Sayoko's smile was radiant. "Okay."

"Race you to the jungle gym—last one there's a rotten egg!" Hisako called as she tagged Sayoko's shoulder and ran towards the playground.

Sayoko looked back at the ants scurrying around the dirt patch. She took a fearful glance over to Hisako, who was still running to the playground with her back turned.

Sayoko stared at the helpless creature in her hand. Deep chin dimples formed at the corners of her mouth as she giggled and placed the butterfly back down into the legion of ants. "Wait for me!"

# Smooth Sailing

THE LIGHT JOSTLING of the JR train didn't usually bother Yoshihiko Sasaki. *I think I'm going to be sick...*

"You okay? You're looking a little green there, bud."

"Shut up, Sato."

It was standing room only, all carriages full to capacity. The number of people increased the summer's heat tenfold, making the air thick and unbearable. Sasaki tried to keep his balance as he held the grab handle in one hand and wiped the sweat dripping down his face with the other.

"I can't believe I'll have to put up with this every day."

"Don't sweat the small stuff. At least you made it this far. Do you have any idea how many others got jobs so quick after leaving the academy? It was only us and a few other guys. So bury the nerves. You got this."

Sato had been Sasaki's best friend at the Prefectural School for Police. Twenty-one months of gruelling martial arts training, written exams, and a lot of late-night drinking. And, of course, putting up with Sato's surprises. Between spiking people's drinks with ketchup or wasabi and pulling faces during sparring matches, Sasaki was surprised the serial practical joker had actually managed to become a policeman.

次は北浦和。北浦和。

*Next stop, Kita-Urawa Station. Kita-Urawa Station.*

"This you?" Sasaki asked as the train came to a stop and the automatic doors slid open. Floods of people exited, filing onto the platform like a wave parting in different directions.

"Sure is. Kita-Urawa Police Station, here I come."

"Now there's a scary thought. Good luck."

"You too. Don't screw up on your first day."

Sasaki stole a seat before a fresh barrage of people came bustling onto the train. The doors slid shut, and the train departed with a resounding whoosh. Sasaki took a deep breath, steeling himself.

*I can't wait for today to be over and done with.*

A woman struggled to keep a firm hold of the vertical rail along the train seats. It was only after a large jolt nearly toppled her over that Sasaki noticed she was heavily pregnant. Sasaki stood and tapped the woman on the shoulder. "Here, take my seat," he said and took hold of the nearest grab handle. The woman's face softened as she bowed her head and thanked him for his kindness.

*Not like I had much of a choice. What would people think if a uniformed police officer didn't offer his seat to a pregnant woman? Even if it wasn't a priority seat, it would've looked bad. At least it's not much longer until my stop...*

次は浦和。浦和。

*Next stop, Urawa Station. Urawa Station.*

Sasaki checked his wristwatch as he got off the train and power-walked to the exit. Urawa Police Station was a seventeen-minute walk from the train station—no time for detours. By the time Sasaki arrived, he felt as if he was burning from the inside out.

*I'd kill for an iced coffee...*

It looked just like any other building; big, industrial, and professional; the only identifying factor being the floral *asahikage* police insignia on the entryway.

Sasaki took a deep breath before pushing through the revolving doors and walking up to the receptionist to sign in. She wasn't much older than him, judging by her appearance. Probably also fresh out of university, but he could see why she'd been hired. She was very easy on the eyes. "Excuse me."

She didn't even look up from her computer before interrupting him. "You must be the new recruit. Welcome.

We look forward to working with you. Someone has already informed me to direct you to Sergeant Oda. He will be your supervising officer from now on. Take the elevator to the first floor to get to the main office. If you need anything, please do not hesitate to ask." Her robotic tone made him feel somewhat unwelcome.

Sasaki's cheeks burned. "Thank you very much. I look forward to working with you," he said as he bowed at a thirty-degree angle. He had practised the set phrase and correct bow the night before, knowing he always became tongue-tied when he was nervous. He didn't want to make a bad first impression.

The upstairs office was open plan, with the officers' desks spread out in increments. Only the inspector had a separate office, and only his was labelled.

*God, where do I start...*

After several minutes of standing there like an idiot, Sasaki finally worked up the courage to ask someone, anyone, where he could find Sergeant Oda; only to be interrupted before he could get a single word out.

"Sasaki, is it?" Sasaki flinched. He hadn't noticed anyone behind him. The man's voice was deep and downright intimidating.

Sasaki spun around, then bowed. "Yes, sir. I'm Yoshihiko Sasaki. It's a pleasure to meet you, sir."

The man was younger than he sounded, with only a few light wrinkles around his eyes and forehead. He couldn't have been any older than forty. "I'm Osamu Oda, nice to meet you. Looks like you'll be with me. Work hard and pay attention, and we'll get along fine." Sergeant Oda gestured for Sasaki to follow him to the elevator. "Come on, we'll start with patrol. You need to know this area better than your own house, so you don't accidentally wander into another station's area of responsibility. I take it they still cover that briefly at the academy?"

"Yes, sir."

"Good."

They took the elevator to the ground floor, Sasaki taking care to follow a few steps behind Sergeant Oda. "Our area of responsibility is limited to Urawa Ward and Minami Ward only; all other areas are someone else's problem, so don't go stepping on any toes," Sergeant Oda explained as they made their way out into the foyer.

An older man, in his late fifties or sixties, came through the door just as they were about the leave. Sergeant Oda sank into a deep bow. "Good morning, Inspector Takeuchi."

"Good morning, Oda. Ah, taking our new recruit out on patrol? Very good. And how's your daughter getting along? Sayoko, isn't it?"

"Yes, sir. She's studying for her entrance exams—medical school," Sergeant Oda said, radiating pride. "She's aspired to be a surgeon since she was in middle school."

"Is that so? Very impressive. I'm sure she'll go on to do great things, just like her father."

"Thank you, sir."

The inspector nodded before taking his leave, Sasaki's

gaze trailing after him. Sasaki hesitated. "If you don't mind my asking, sir, but how long have you been a policeman?"

Sergeant Oda chuckled. "Ten years. It sounds like a lot, but you'll be surprised how fast it goes. There's a lot to do, though I admit most of it isn't overly exciting. But it is necessary. We're incredibly lucky to work in such a low-crime area. It reflects the effort we put into our work. Keep your eyes and mind wide open. Remember: Just because you don't see something, doesn't mean it's not there."

"I understand, sir." Sasaki held his hands over his eyes, blocking out the blazing morning sun.

*Well, that's a cheery way to start the morning...*

# LIVE AND LEARN

BEEP-BEEP!

Sayoko's cell phone vibrated in her skirt pocket. She flipped it open under her desk, trying to be discreet since it was the middle of class. It was from Hisako.

Hey, Sayoko! ( *′▽`*) My mom's stuck at work, so I have
to pick up Satoru from school then start dinner, so I can't
go to Sakuragi Library with you after school today (т─т)
Sorry!

Sayoko sighed. Commuting wasn't as much fun alone. By the time she arrived at the library, her motivation had plummeted. The information in the medical books was confusing and hard to remember, jumbling around in her head and getting lost in the Bermuda Triangle of her mind.

*Forget passing the entrance exam... If I can't fix this, I won't be able to keep up even if I get in,* Sayoko thought as she slammed her books shut and returned them to the shelves.

*Maybe I need a more practical approach...* She headed back to Ōmiya Station.

The station was packed with people. Everyone walked with a purpose—quickly and barely taking the time to register each other's existence as they ran to catch their trains or meandered from shop to shop.

Sayoko moved with the flow of people, following the signs to the platform heading to Yono Station.

*It's like the flow of blood through a body.* Even the layout of the station resembled anatomy: If the yellow grooved floor tiles to lead the blind were the veins, then the corridors were the blood vessels, and the platforms, the internal organs. A group of elementary school kids raced past Sayoko, knocking her bag out of her hand when they bumped into her. They didn't even stop to apologise.

*Rotten little shits...* They'd kicked her bag along the floor towards the restrooms. They all looked her right in the eye before laughing and running away. Sayoko cursed under her breath and went to get her satchel. It was only after she crouched forwards to pick it up that she noticed a boarded-up area tucked away in an alcove behind the restrooms. It wasn't visible from any other angle, only from up close. She'd been through Ōmiya Station hundreds of times and had never seen it before. Sheets of old plywood overlapped, haphazardly nailed together as if the person had been drunk when they boarded it up, with "RESTRICTED AREA" spray painted diagonally in large, somewhat faded, characters.

*I wonder where this leads to*, Sayoko thought, her heart pounding. The sound of an ascending scale of a xylophone blasted over the intercom.

まもなく、一番線に与野駅方面行きがまいります。

*The train bound for Yono Station will arrive momentarily at Platform One.*

危ないですから黄色い線までお下がりください。

*Please wait behind the yellow line.*

*Damn, that's my train!* Sayoko bolted to Platform One, slipping down the stairs before catching herself on the handrail.

"Hey! Wait for me!"

"No, it's this way."

"Hurry up!" Children screamed and shouted as they pushed past her so they could slip onto the train first and steal any available seats.

Sayoko clicked her teeth. She squeezed past people in the over-filled train car and tried to find a grab handle. The train jolted forwards as it left the station. Adults knew to be quiet and to not disturb others on their commute, but the group of kids killed what would have otherwise been a peaceful journey. *They're like a swarm of locusts.* Sayoko found it hard to drown out their chattering, which was only made worse when two boys started climbing the rails framing the seats, seeing who could do the most chin ups, while the others burst into fits of laughter. The other passengers looked just as annoyed as she did. *Make that a pack of wild animals. How can their parents just let them loose like this?*

She'd never really thought about it before, but there were hardly any children accompanied by their parents, or any adult, going to and from school. They were given so much leeway.

次は**与野**。**与野**。

*Next stop, Yono Station. Yono Station.*

Sayoko got off the train and moved with the flow of people again, towards the West Exit. She got out her cell phone to let her mother know she'd be home soon.

Long shadows stretched over Yono Park as the sun started to set, casting a warm golden-orange light. Sayoko stopped just shy of her front door, unable to tear herself away. It was like the monarch butterfly's wings.

She set down her satchel, removed her bento box, and crossed the road to the park. It was deserted. She knelt at the base of a nearby tree, scanning the area before finding what she needed and scooping it into her lunch box.

After a quick hello to her mother, Sayoko practically

skipped up the stairs to her bedroom, fastening the deadlock firmly in place so she wouldn't be disturbed. She took out a large tray and put it on her desk.

Her lunch box took centre stage.

When she was younger, Sayoko had aspired to be a manga artist. But it turned out she wasn't any good at drawing, no matter how much she practised. She still had all her old supplies tucked away in one of her desk drawers, including a precision blade used for cutting screen tones.

The array of insects decorating Sayoko's walls peered down at her, silent witnesses as she removed the lid to her lunchbox and carefully removed its occupant: a lone praying mantis. Sayoko cupped her hand over it so it couldn't fly away, cocking her head to the side while she inspected it.

*Mom always says fresh ingredients are best.*

A small tin of silver pins sat at the right side of Sayoko's desk, for mounting her specimens. She took four pins and stabbed them through each arm and the lower part of the mantis' torso so she could get to work. The exacto blade made an excellent scalpel. Ever so slowly, she sliced off one of its front legs, talking herself through the process of amputation she had read at the library earlier.

"First, make an incision around the part to be amputated. The intended appendage is to be removed, and the bone smoothed; except in this case, where the patient has no bone." The leg fell to one side, making a slight crunch under the pressure of the blade. Sayoko set down the blade and lifted the delicate wing on its back. She gave it a light tug, plucking it excruciatingly slowly from the creature's body.

It came away easily. She placed the dismembered wing to the side and continued cutting the live mantis apart, piece by piece. "A flap is then constructed of muscle, connective tissue, and skin to cover the raw end of the bone. The flap is closed over with sutures, which will remain for one month. Interesting that despite having no form of anaesthetic, the subject shows no signs of pain or distress."

By the time she was done, all that remained of the mantis was its head and torso. It twitched occasionally, and the torso wriggled and writhed as it made a slight hissing noise from its abdomen. *Perhaps it's wondering why it can't feel its legs.* Sayoko took out a thick notebook and polaroid camera and snapped the shutter with a click and a whirr.

*Can it even feel pain? Its eyes look empty, like little green almonds...* She glued the picture onto the first page of her notebook and wrote the date along with the 'case notes.' Taking the mantis' head between her left thumb and forefinger, she lifted it from the tray, inching her hands further apart. The hissing got louder and louder the further she pulled, followed by a tiny crunch as its head separated from its body.

Its eyes looked no different from when it was alive.

Sayoko finished her notes, then slid the mantis' remains into the wastebasket under her desk, along with some papers to hide it. Sayoko sighed, her lips down turned into a bored pout. *I couldn't practise half of what I wanted to on that paper-thin skin...*

A scratching at her window tore her from her thoughts, followed by a familiar meow.

A grin crept across Sayoko's face. She slid the window up and petted the cat's head.

"What are you doing all the way over here, Mochi?" Sayoko said in her usual baby tone. "Hisako will be worried sick about you." She tenderly picked him up, bringing him inside, and slid the window shut.

# LOST AND FOUND

"MOCHIII! HERE KITTY."

Hisako shook a box of Mochi's favourite cat food. He didn't usually wander very far, so he'd always come running as soon as he heard it. "Where the heck is he?"

She put the box back in the kitchen and stared down at his empty bowl. It was the first thing she'd bought for him when he was just a kitten—white glossy ceramic with fish bones and cat pawprints printed in thick black along the side. "I'm sure he's fine, sweetie. He's probably just wandering around trying to find a pretty kitty to make kittens with." Hisako's mother chuckled.

"It's been three days already… and he always comes when I call him." Mochi had been her eleventh birthday present from her father. Hisako kept the photo on her dresser: her holding up this little white kitten, a strawberry shortcake with candles on the table, and her dad smiling with his arms around her. It was one of the few photos they had of him after he lost all his hair, aside from the one of him holding Satoru after he was born. He had been so self-conscious about his haggard appearance (like a zombie, he used to say), and of the oxygen tubes. But despite that, it was one of Hisako's happiest memories. She liked to think that her father watched over her through Mochi's eyes. "Hisako!"

"What?"

"Didn't you hear me calling you? Sayoko's at the door," her mother said, tearing Hisako from her thoughts.

Sayoko looked lovely and summery in a long white sundress and wide-rimmed beach hat with a chiffon bow. Hisako had always secretly envied Sayoko's looks, not that she'd ever admit it. She felt so frumpy in comparison. Sayoko's pale skin, doe eyes, and long silky hair would always be popular with boys. *If only she'd ditch the glasses.*

"Good morning, Hisako." Sayoko walked into the kitchen and glanced down at Mochi's empty bowl, her forehead creasing. "Mochi still isn't back yet?"

Hisako grabbed her bag and swung it onto her shoulder. "Come on. We'll be late for cram school."

Hisako tried not to cry as she and Sayoko walked home. She'd been thinking about Mochi through the entire class, and the more she thought, the more she worried. *What if he*

*got hit by a car and is lying somewhere on the side of the road?* Hisako felt something brush against her palm. Sayoko held out a piece of paper, sneaking it into Hisako's hand. "What's this?" she asked, reading it aloud.

LOST CAT

White, male Persian with blue collar, answers to the name

'Mochi'

Lost 3 days ago near Yono Park.

If you have any information, please contact:

HISAKO NAKAMURA: h.n@softbank.jp

Hisako gawked at Sayoko.

"I printed them yesterday while I was at the library. Thought they might help," Sayoko said, smiling sweetly at her. "I know how much he means to you."

It was comforting to know she had a friend who knew her better than anyone else; what she was thinking, how she was feeling. She never had to explain herself, not to Sayoko.

Tears rolled down Hisako's cheeks as she pulled Sayoko into a hug. "You're the best friend I've ever had."

Sayoko passed Hisako her pocket handkerchief so she could wipe her face, then took two handfuls of posters out of her bag. "Let's put them up on the way home—kill two birds with one stone, yeah?"

"Yeah. Thanks," Hisako replied, her voice nasal from crying.

"What are friends for?"

# 7

## Tantalising Temptations

"DON'T FORGET TO copy down this formula on the board—it'll be on next week's test, so make sure you know it." *Urgh. Great, more math,* Sayoko thought as the math teacher left the classroom. Chair and table legs screeched as students shifted from one place to another, moving tables around so they could sit in groups for lunch.

Hisako pulled over a chair and took a seat at Sayoko's desk. "What have you got for lunch today?"

"*Tamagoyaki, tako* sausages, fried fish, and a rice-ball. You?"

"Leftover hamburg steak—nothing fancy. Can I bum a sausage?" Hisako asked, already leaning over the desk, chopsticks poised to steal one of the little sausages cut up to look like a four-legged octopus.

"Go on, then."

"Yay! *Itadakimasu*," Hisako said, giving thanks before eating the unsuspecting octopus whole.

Sayoko chuckled before saying grace and digging into her own lunch. "Did anyone contact you with info about Mochi? No one's seen him yet?" Sayoko asked between mouthfuls of rice and salad.

"No, not yet. But it's only been a week since we put the signs up. It'll only be a matter of time. I just need to be patient."

Sayoko's mind wandered back to the last time she saw Mochi, while she ate her lunch: removing his collar and massaging his neck as she held him down. A juicy piece of fish, cooked to perfection. Cutting off his tail and practising her sutures: A large bite of rice ball. Slicing through his foot and watching the blood stain his white fur as he screamed and hissed through the duct tape: A mouthful of rolled omelette. Wrapping his mutilated carcase in a weighted bag and disposing of it in the Kamo River: putting her chopsticks and lunchbox away and wiping her mouth with a napkin.

Sayoko's smile was as warm and comforting as it always was when she spoke to Hisako. "Try not to worry too much. I'm sure he'll turn up soon." She was glad that Hisako couldn't read her mind. It would be unfortunate to lose such a good friend over something as trivial as a pet.

*Besides, it was for a good cause; I needed a bigger test subject. It's just an animal. She'll get over it.*

Sayoko read her medical book while she waited for the train bound for Urawa Station; Saitama Nursing School was only a short walk from there.

*It's not really a university, but it might still be worth a look.*

The voice over the intercom announced the arrival of the train bound for Urawa and the other train going in the opposite direction on Platform Two. A little girl with blond hair tied in pigtails ran across the platform, bumping into Sayoko on the way.

"Oh, I'm sorry," she said, bowing her head slightly.

*At least this one has some manners*, Sayoko thought, forcing a smile. "It's alright."

Sayoko took the pencil tucked behind her ear and made notes in her textbook as the little girl raced onto the train going in the opposite direction to Urawa.

Sayoko glanced back at the train heading to Urawa.

"Excuse me, please," she called, running to the opposite side of the platform. She squeezed past the standing passengers and found a vacant seat. The little blond girl didn't even look up from her Nintendo console when Sayoko sat across from her. Sayoko continued reading her book, only occasionally peeking up at her.

The little girl only looked about seven years old and had pink ribbons in her hair.

*She must be half Japanese. No parent in their right mind would let a child that young bleach their hair.*

A baby's screams followed the sound of something plastic rolling along the vinyl floor of the train. Half the passengers shot the mother a dirty look. *In their eyes it was inconsiderate enough bringing that thing on the train at all, let alone in that enormous pram. Being a parent seems like more trouble than it's worth.*

The baby's rattle rolled along the floor until it hit the little girl's pink Mary-Jane shoes, distracting her from her game. The girl put her game safely in her bag, picked up the rattle and went over to the distressed mother.

"Here you go. I think he dropped this." She waved the rattle in front of the baby's face, giggling as he snatched it from her. "Aw, he's so cute!"

The mother nodded her head in thanks, and the little girl returned to her seat across from Sayoko.

次は土呂。土呂。

*Next stop, Toro Station. Toro Station.*

お出口は左側です。

*Doors will open on the left-hand side.*

The little girl stopped, looking from side to side as she tried to remember her lefts and rights. The doors opened, and she followed the other passengers exiting the train.

閉まるドーアにご注意ください。

*The train doors are now closing.*

The train jostled as it slowly left the station, but when it picked up speed, the journey became so smooth that Sayoko could take notes with perfectly straight lines.

Taking the pencil from behind her ear, she wrote two words in the margin of her book: Toro Station.

# Pink Sequin Shoes

MIYUKI SKIPPED DOWN the familiar path home from Toro Station singing the theme song from *Doraemon* while she hurried home. Grown-ups chuckled when they passed her, but she didn't care.

Taking a short-cut through Fujimi Park, she hopped from paving stone to paving stone, trying not to stand on the cracks. There wasn't much of a playground there—only a tiny plastic thing for babies and toddlers to crawl through. Even the slide was small and plastic. *I wish we had a real playground around here*, Miyuki thought as she waited for the crossing man to turn green.

One more crossing and she'd be home.

"I'm hooome!" Miyuki called, kicking her shoes off in the entryway and running into the living room and turning on the TV. The same *Doraemon* theme song she'd been singing all the way home played loudly from the speakers.

Miyuki sat so close to the screen that her breath fogged it up. "Welcome home. Miyuki! What have I told you about sitting that close to the TV? Turn it off, please," her mom said, hands on her hips. Miyuki's dad sat at the dining table, looking at her over the top of his glasses. Her mom's hair was blond, like Miyuki's, and her accent was a mixture of Canadian-English and Japanese.

"But Mommy—" Miyuki whined.

"It's not a punishment. Your father and I have a surprise for you." Her mom smiled. "We've been waiting for you to get home."

Miyuki's dad put his papers to one side and removed his glasses. "Come now, don't you want to know what it is?"

Miyuki's face lit up. "A surprise?" She switched off the TV and bounced over to the dining table. "What is it? What is it?" she asked, her hands on the table as she hopped in place.

"Now, now, you're not a rabbit." Her mother laughed. She took a box from behind her back and put it on the table. It was wrapped in baby pink polka-dotted paper with a bright pink ribbon.

Miyuki shuffled from foot to foot and giggled. "But my birthday's not until next month."

Her parents chuckled. "We know that, dear. This is for being a good girl. You've been such a big girl taking the train by yourself to and from school, and your teacher told us about the test you took the other day—you got a perfect score. That deserves a reward." Her dad looked so proud of her. "At this rate, you'll have no trouble getting into a good middle school."

"Well done, sweetheart," her mom said, kissing the top of her head. Their Shiba Inu, Shiro, was at her feet, his tail waggling and mouth hanging open as if he was smiling, too.

Miyuki undid the ribbon and ripped through the wrapping paper, revealing a shoe box.

"I think I know what it is!" she squealed.

She tore the lid off and pulled out the tissue paper. It was the pink sequin shoes she'd been wanting for weeks, in an adorable Mary-Jane style with a small heel and ankle straps in shiny metallic pink. Her favourite part was the little heart and star-shaped sequins sprinkled over the main shoe and the moon-shaped pendant with rhinestones attached to the buckle. Her classmates would be so jealous.

"Thank you, thank you, thank you!" she squeaked, jumping up and down and hugging the shoes to her chest. She put them on right away. They went beautifully with her lace ankle socks and her favourite pink hair ribbons.

"You're welcome, sweetie. Take good care of them."

"Can I go take Shiro for his walk?" Miyuki asked. She couldn't wait to show off her new shoes.

"By yourself?" her mom asked, her forehead knitted with concern. She glanced at Miyuki's dad, and he nodded.

"If she's old enough to take the train by herself, then she's old enough to walk Shiro, too," he said before turning to Miyuki. "But not too far, alright? Stay in the area."

Miyuki nodded furiously. "I promise, Daddy."

"If you're sure, dear…" Miyuki's mom said before attaching Shiro's lead to his leather collar and taking out her cell phone. "Now, I need a picture before you go. Say 'cheese.'"

Miyuki held Shiro's lead and held her hand up in a peace sign. "Cheese!"

Miyuki walked Shiro through the park where he stopped at every bush and tree to sniff around.

"Cut it out, Shiro!" she whined, tugging on the lead.

There were hardly any people around. "Maybe there's a festival or something nearby. Should we go see?"

Suddenly, Shiro started to growl. His shoulders hunched over and his head lowered, lips curled into a snarl. The fur on the back of his neck stood up. "What, you don't like that idea? You lazy doggie."

"Hi there."

A lady was sitting on one of the park benches; not an older lady like her mommy, but then, she didn't look like a kid either. She was wearing makeup, including cute pink lip gloss and her nails had adorable 3D decals stuck on them—bows, cupcakes, and cookies. Maybe she was a model.

"Hi," Miyuki said, staring at the lady through her eyelashes. Strangers made her feel shy.

"What are you doing out here all by yourself?" the lady said, glancing from Miyuki to Shiro. "That's a really cute dog you have there. What's his name?" Her voice was beautiful, and she had the prettiest hair Miyuki had ever seen, coppery-red with shoulder-length ringlets.

"Shiro."

"That's a nice name. Is it because he's white?" The lady giggled, leaving her seat to crouch in front of the growling dog. "Hi Shiro, my name's Natsumi." She held her hand out for him to sniff, and he slowly relaxed, giving her hand a tentative lick.

"He likes you." Miyuki crouched next to her. "That's good. He doesn't usually growl like that."

"It's okay. Most dogs are like that around strangers. They're amazing animals. They can tell all sorts of things about a person just by their smell. Their instincts tell them if they're good or bad," Natsumi said, petting Shiro's head and under his chin. He was still a little stiff, but didn't seem to mind the attention.

"Wow. I didn't know that."

"It's true. I'm training to be a vet, so I know a lot about animals. I can tell you really like them, too. He's a beautiful dog. You obviously take really good care of him." Natsumi's smile only made her more beautiful. Her eyes sparkled with an unusual green-gold shimmer.

"Um… can I ask you something?" Miyuki asked, trying to overcome her shyness.

"Of course."

"Is that your real hair and eye colour?"

Natsumi cocked her head to the side, smiling as she stared at Miyuki's hair. "Absolutely. What about yours?"

Miyuki nodded. "My mommy's from Canada."

"Well, you're very lucky. Lots of girls pay a lot of money to get hair like yours. I bet you're really popular at school."

Miyuki looked at the ground, scratching behind Shiro's ear. She couldn't look Natsumi in the eye. "...Not really. The other kids are mean to me."

"I see. Kids can be mean, but try not to let them get to you. My classmates made fun of me, too, when I was young. Just ignore them. They're only mean because they're jealous." Natsumi stood, her hand firmly clasped around Shiro's lead. "I like your shoes, by the way."

Miyuki's cheeks went bright red. "Thank you. My mommy and daddy gave them to me after school today."

"Wow, your parents sound really nice. You're such a lucky girl."

*I hope I look as pretty as her when I'm older*, Miyuki thought, noticing how Natsumi's smile made her whole face glow.

"You know, I have just the thing to stop those kids making fun of you. It worked like magic for me."

"Really? What is it?" Miyuki asked, but Natsumi simply put a finger to her lips.

"It's a secret. If anyone else found out, then they'd all want it, or try to steal it. If you come with me, I'll give it to you. I can tell you deserve it, and I don't need it anymore."

Miyuki looked back towards her house. "Mommy and Daddy will want me to be home soon..."

"I don't live very far from here—just one or two stations away. I'll pay for your train fare, too. We could be there and back in five minutes, I promise."

"What about Shiro? He can't go on a train."

"He'll be perfectly safe tied up outside the station. We'll be back in no time at all." Natsumi held out her hand.

Miyuki took it and put her other hand through the loop at the end of Shiro's lead, wrapping it around so she had a firm grip on it. "Okay."

Miyuki's heart pounded with excitement as she walked hand in hand with Natsumi. She couldn't wait for school tomorrow. No one would ever be mean to her again.

# LOST

"URAWA POLICE STATION, what's your emergency?"

Sasaki stifled a snicker at this set phrase, considering the most urgent cases he had dealt with in the past month were a stolen handbag and a lost student ID.

His smirk quickly faded. Taking a pen and paper, he wrote as many details as he could as the woman spoke to him over the phone.  "Yes, ma'am. We will be there shortly. Please try to remain calm."

Sasaki found Sergeant Oda in the break room with a hot cup of coffee. "Excuse me, sir? We have a missing child case, sir. Suspected kidnapping." Sasaki had tried to keep his voice calm and dispassionate but had failed miserably. Even he could hear it shaking.

Sergeant Oda's chair squealed against the vinyl floor

when he stood and marched straight to the door. "Let's go. Do you have the address?"

"Yes, sir. It's Near Urawa Station."

"When did you last see your son, Mrs Watanabe?" Sergeant Oda asked, his face neutral and voice impartial.

Sasaki could feel sweat dripping down his neck, and he tried not to fidget as they sat on the sofa. Both parents had deep-set bags under their eyes.

"Yesterday. He didn't come home from school, so we thought something must have happened there. We went to the Warabi Police Station—Daiichi goes to Kawaguchi Shiritsu Shibaminami Elementary School, near Warabi Station." Mrs Watanabe cried as her husband put his arms around her. She was clutching a small toy to her chest: A white lion in a baseball uniform. "The West Exit has a police box right there. How did they miss him?" She burst into hysterical sobs.

"If you don't mind my asking, why did you wait so long before contacting the police?"

Mr Watanabe's brow furrowed. Removing his arm from around his wife's shoulders, he leaned forward in his chair; an intimidating gesture, given the man's height and build.

"You think we *wanted* to wait this long? We spent hours explaining the situation to the police in Warabi, only to be told later to contact you instead, since we live near Urawa." The man's cheeks flushed with anger. "We spent half the time playing phone tag with the police, trying to figure out whose jurisdiction it came under."

"I see… I'm sorry to hear that. We'll do our best to find your son. Can you tell us more about him? We'll need some details before we can conduct a search—age, hair colour, scars, birthmarks. Anything you think of could help with our search," Sergeant Oda said. It amazed Sasaki that he could stay so calm, given the circumstances. His voice was steady as stone.

"He's seven, has short black hair, no birthmarks or scars," Mrs Watanabe said, passing Sergeant Oda a photo. "He was wearing a white T-shirt with a Pokémon character on it the day he disappeared." Her eyes looked as if they would swell shut if she cried any more.

Mr Watanabe pointed to the photo. "He was also wearing that Seibu Lions baseball cap. He wore it every day. I got it for him when we went to see them in Tokyo for the Japan series. It was his birthday. He was so happy. It was the first time they'd won in years."

Sasaki inspected the photo: It was obviously a school photo taken at the playground. The cap was one size too big, lolling off to the side, but the bright red visor made it stand out. Whoever took the picture had caught the boy mid-laugh, his mouth wide open in a grin, revealing three missing teeth.

*Someone had to have seen that cap*, Sasaki thought. He furiously took notes while Sergeant Oda continued asking questions.

"He went to and from school by train, is that correct? Would he go alone or with a group of friends?"

"With friends. But we called their parents when he didn't come home and they said that the kids didn't see anything," Mr Watanabe replied.

"Could you give us their names, please? And the route he took to and from school."

"Of course."

Sergeant Oda glanced towards the stairs. "Would it be possible to see his room? It may give us some insight."

"Up the stairs, first door on the right," Mr Watanabe replied. "Take your time."

Sasaki's shoulders deflated. Daiichi Watanabe's room looked just like any other small child's: heart-breakingly innocent. It was wall-to-wall red, white, and navy—the colours of the Saitama Seibu Lions baseball team—and was full of baseball memorabilia: signed T-shirts, baseball gloves, and dozens of Leo-Lion and Lina-Lion toys. The bed was unmade, as if it had just been slept in; the rocket-ship bedspread wrinkled and tossed to the side.

Toy cars, action figures, and crayon drawings in various stages of completion littered the floor. Sergeant Oda began scanning the room for any clues, so Sasaki followed suit.

Sasaki picked up a piece of paper at Daiichi's desk. A half-finished drawing of a person playing baseball was at the top, and the bottom half was a *genkō-yōshi* grid for describing his drawing. The handwriting was messy, obviously a child's, written only in hiragana. Sasaki remembered having to write similar essays in elementary school. "'When I grow up, I want to play pro baseball and join the Seibu Lions and marry Ms Saki.'" Sasaki read aloud. "Ha, cute. He certainly was a Seibu Lions fan. I wonder who Ms Saki is…"

"Try not to use the past tense in front of the parents, Sasaki." Sergeant Oda peeked over Sasaki's shoulder at the drawing. "Come on. We'll need to put in some serious overtime on this one. We've already lost half a day."

By the time they had questioned all of Daiichi's teachers, classmates, and friends, children were flocking to the school gate to go home. Sasaki and Sergeant Oda both bowed deeply, thanking the teachers for their time.

"I'm sorry we couldn't be of more help. I hope you find him soon," said Ms Saki, Daiichi's homeroom teacher.

Sasaki grinned. *I can see why the kid liked her.* Her voice was feminine and sweet; he could've listened to her for hours. And she was gorgeous, with a peaches-and-cream complexion, plump glossy lips, and beautiful wavy copper hair. *Just my type.*

"Sasaki?" Sergeant Oda's booming voice snapped Sasaki from his thoughts.

"Yes, sir?"

"Done daydreaming? I asked if you got all that. Break it

down and read it back to me. Let's see if we're on the same page." He raised an eyebrow.

Sasaki cleared his throat, suddenly nervous. "So, according to his teacher, Ms Saki Sakurabi, Daiichi stayed later than usual to practise baseball the day he disappeared. This correlates with the statements given by his friends, who said that they left before him." Sasaki madly flipped from page to page of his pocket notebook, his throat dry and croaky. "He would usually commute home with them since they all live in the same neighbourhood, taking the train from Warabi Station to Urawa Station.

Apparently, he stayed behind to practise because he wants to try out for the baseball club when he enters middle school; he wanted to get an early start. Ms Saki saw him leave after five o'clock, before they locked up for the day. She asked if she could walk him home, but he declined, so he couldn't have been nabbed near the school. There would have been witnesses."

"Good. Any leads from that alone? Where do we go from here?" Sergeant Oda asked as they left through the school gate. Sasaki thought he saw him crack a smile at the wide-eyed stares they were getting from the kids. It must be quite scary for police to show up at their school, especially at that age.

*He's testing me.*

"No, sir. Nothing sounds suspicious so far. Maybe something will turn up at Warabi Station if we show his photo around?"

Sergeant Oda smiled, a flash of pride in his eyes. "Very good. Let's go."

Sasaki finally exhaled.

"Excuse me, did you see this boy coming through here between five and six p.m. this past Tuesday?" Sasaki asked the workers at Warabi Station police box, near the West Exit. The men snorted. Only one of them leaned over to get a closer look at the photo, a young man in his early twenties.

"Do you have any idea how many kids pass through here every hour? It would be impossible to remember them all."

"Try." Sergeant Oda nodded his head to the other men. The younger man took the hint and passed the picture to his colleagues, but they all shook their heads.

"Sorry. All kids around that age look the same to me."

Sasaki clicked his teeth. "What about the cap? Recognise it at all?"

"Not that I remember. What about you guys?" They all just shook their heads, only half listening; either getting back to work or resuming their breaks, reading manga.

"It's bright red. How the hell could you miss it?" Sasaki snapped, clicking his teeth again, louder this time.

"Hey, it's not our job to check out what people are wearing. We just make sure no one gets through without buying a ticket first. If the kid had a ticket or Suika pre-paid pass card, we would have no reason to notice him. And we would have noticed anyone suspicious. The officers from Warabi Police already checked out the security cameras. It was clean. Nothing out of the ordinary."

"Bet you'd have noticed if it was a pretty high school girl we were looking for," Sasaki hissed.

"What did you just say?" the young officer said, sliding his chair out from under him; his lip curled, and his hand formed a fist.

"Alright, alright—that's enough." Sergeant Oda grasped Sasaki's shoulders and pushed him back, tilting his head slightly to the station workers. "Thank you for your time."

Sergeant Oda raised his eyebrows at Sasaki, making him feel like a wounded dog.

"Sorry, sir. They were our last hope. Now we're just at another dead end…" Sasaki trailed off, holding his fingers to his temples as if simply rubbing them would melt the stress away. "It's hard when it's such a little kid."

Sergeant Oda sighed, his face softening. "I understand. I'm a father, after all. No matter how big they get, you never really stop seeing them like little Daiichi here." He held up the photo, an almost tangible sadness creeping across his face. "Don't worry, we'll find him." He scanned his train pass to get onto the platform, Sasaki following close behind. "People don't just evaporate into thin air."

# Just a Dream

MIYUKI ROLLED OVER in her sleep, wondering why her soft fluffy bed was hurting her back. Something sharp and pointy stabbed at her; cold, like metal. She wanted to wake up and move it, but her eyes felt so heavy. She could barely lift them, and what little she could see was blurry.

"Mommy…?" She tried to speak, but nothing came out. Her mouth wouldn't open. It was covered with something sticky. *I feel sick*, she thought, tears streaming down her cheeks. She couldn't remember how she got there. She remembered her parents giving her a present, then taking Shiro for a walk, but the rest was blank or fuzzy, like a dream.

Hair tickled her neck—one of her pigtails must have fallen out. She blinked the tears out of her eyes and tried to sit up, but her wrists were tied behind her back with the same sticky stuff covering her mouth. Without the strength to stand, Miyuki flopped back onto her back.

*What's that smell?* she thought, scrunching up her nose and dry retching through the tape, willing herself not to throw up.

After what felt like hours, her vision cleared enough to kind of make out where she was. It was dark; the only light being dim strip lights making fizzling sounds when they flashed on and off. Miyuki hoped they wouldn't go out altogether. She was scared of the dark and still used a night-light. As her eyes adjusted to the darkness, she realised she was lower than everything else. Two metal rods ran along the floor.

*Train tracks?* She rolled over onto her side and propped herself up with her elbow, finally managing to sit up after a few tries. The stones covering the track crunched under her weight. Water dripping from the ceiling had made them slick, and she squealed as she slipped and fell headfirst onto something squishy. The bad smell intensified, as did the sound of buzzing flies. Miyuki wished her hands were free so she could wipe whatever it was off her face. It was wet and slimy and smelt worse than anything she had smelt before. She wriggled into a sitting position, then felt it wasn't just wet—some parts were soft, like matted fur.

Everything came into focus as her eyes adjusted more; the flickering lights illuminating the squishy muck. Shiro's once white fur was now almost completely red. His ears had been cut off and were lying next to him on the ground, along with the end of his snout. His stomach had been cut wide open and pulled over, like a freshly made bed, waiting to be tucked in. He didn't even look like a dog anymore.

Miyuki screamed, the duct tape puffing in and out as she hyperventilated. She backed away as fast as she could with her hands and feet still bound. Something warm trickled down her legs, drenching her skirt.

She curled into a ball and sobbed as the world around her spun before finally going black.

A bright light pricking her eyelids woke Miyuki from a deep, restless sleep. The lights weren't flickering anymore.

She must have been asleep for a long time; her skirt and underwear were dry, and her arms were starting to cramp. The memories came flooding back, and tears filled her eyes as she saw Shiro's body in better lighting.

He smelt even worse than before.

*I'm scared. I want to go home.* Miyuki squeezed her eyes shut, hoping she'd be back home when she opened them.

When she re-opened them, she was still on the train tracks. The ground trembled beneath her, and the sound of trains rumbled through the room, puffs of dust floating down from the ceiling.

*Trains ... a train station?* She wondered when she suddenly remembered something: Natsumi.

She had gone on the subway with a lady she met at the

park. She'd been really nice and bought her train ticket and a drink since there was no air conditioning on the train. Maybe Natsumi was here too.

Maybe she could help her escape.

Miyuki rolled onto her side and propped herself up on her elbows, closer to the platform this time, so she had something to lean on. She stood, though she was not much taller than the platform. There was no way she could climb up with her hands tied, but at least now she could see the rest of the area. It looked just like any normal subway platform, only dirtier. Even with the lights on, it was darker than normal. Graffiti covered the walls, and everything seemed to be falling apart, like a haunted house. What made it even scarier was that it looked like no one had been down there in a long time.

Further from the tracks, near one of the tiled support pillars on the platform, Miyuki could see the corner of something blue, like a tablecloth on a table. She hopped along the tracks to get a better angle.

The further she went, the more she could see.

It was a boy, sleeping on a table, half covered by a shiny blue blanket, the kind her daddy would take camping. There was a pile of clothes on the ground next to him. All she could make out was a dirty white T-shirt and a baseball cap.

"MMmmMMmmffF!" Miyuki screamed. She'd meant to say, "Help! I'm over here," but the tape muffled her words into soft mumbles. She kept trying anyway. Maybe it would be enough to wake him up.

Miyuki kept hopping along until she finally got a better view. Then she stopped, bracing herself on the platform ledge before slumping back down onto the tracks, almost throwing up what little remained in her stomach.

The boy wasn't sleeping. If it even was a boy.

She couldn't stop violently shivering as she curled back into a ball and cried.

# IGNORANCE IS BLISS

*AH! THAT'S MY TRAIN*, Akira thought, getting squashed as he pushed his way through the crowd. People could see his little red school hat, but they hardly ever got out of the way.

The train doors were closing. He sprinted as fast as he could, but by the time he reached the platform, it was already pulling away from the station.

"Awww…" he said, kicking the ground and scrunching his face up into a pout. He removed his school hat and shoved it into his bag, then took out his Nintendo DS to play Pokémon while he waited for the next train.

*Now I'm glad I snuck it into my bag while Mom wasn't looking,* he thought, glancing around for a seat. They were all taken, apart from one next to a girl reading a big book.

"Do you mind if I sit here?" he asked. She had a pencil

tucked behind her ear and she had super long, straight black hair, like the character from 'Ring.'

She looked at him over the top of her thick-rimmed glasses. "Not at all." Her smile made him feel all warm and fuzzy inside—it made her look way less creepy. He had to go on tippy-toes and do a little hop-jump to sit up on the chair; his feet dangling over the end. His second-hand, Bulbasaur blue game console had a tiny crack in the screen, but it still worked just fine.

The next time he glanced over at her, the girl had put her book down and taken her cell phone out of her bag. She punched the numbers in quickly, one after the other. Akira leaned over slightly to get a better look at what she was typing.

Sorry! Ⅲ( °△° )Ⅲ I'm just catching my last train from Mxxxxxxx I should be back soon ( ´ ▽ ` )｡o　　　❤

It had some *kanji* characters he couldn't read, but it was so cool that she had a cell phone. He'd always wanted one, but his mom said he couldn't have one until he was in middle school, which was forever away. She was so mean.

まもなく、二番線に北朝霞駅方面行きがまいります。

*The train bound for Kita-Asaka will arrive momentarily at Platform Two.*

危ないですから黄色い線までお下がりください。

*Please wait behind the yellow line.*

Akira leaped from his seat and ran to the yellow line, determined not to miss it this time. If he was too late getting home, he'd be scolded. Or worse.

The girl went back to reading her book and Akira boarded the train, nabbing a seat by a window. He crouched on the seat and stared out the window back at the girl on the platform. As the train announcer warned them of the closing doors, he saw the girl take the pencil from behind her ear and write something in her book.

She looked up at him and waved goodbye, with the same sweet smile on her face.

*I can't wait to grow up...*

# FATAL FLAW

SASAKI COLLAPSED INTO one of the hard plastic chairs in the break room, loosening his tie and running his hands through his hair as he leaned back.

*This is a freaking nightmare...*

Another full day of searching, questioning, and interviewing; squat. The only person who thought she'd seen Daiichi was an old woman who was practically blind.

*It could have been any kid wearing a red-rimmed cap.* Sasaki didn't want to go home to a dark, empty apartment. He was depressed enough as it was.

His stomach twisted into knots at the thought of Mr and Mrs Watanabe coming home every day to the empty space left by their missing son. At the dinner table, watching TV; seeing all the kids in their long-sleeved kimono for the year

7-5-3 celebrations. Everything would remind them of what they'd lost. It felt as if a dark cloud had swallowed him, with no way out.

"You alright over there, Sasaki?"

Sasaki removed his hands from his face to find Sergeant Oda staring down at him, concerned.

"Yes, sir. Just tired, is all," Sasaki replied, straightening himself up. He couldn't let anyone on the force know the case was getting to him. They'd think he couldn't handle the pressure.

"It's okay to talk about it," Sergeant Oda said. His smile was gentle and comforting. "It's one hell of a first case to be assigned. You'll go insane if you bottle it all up. The thoughts that go round in your head can become toxic."

Sasaki couldn't look at him. His cheeks burned and he felt ashamed. Tears stung his eyes, but he couldn't let them fall. "What if we never find him?" he asked, his voice shaking. It didn't feel right saying it out loud. Like a bad omen.

"What if they never get that closure? It's fine for us—he just becomes another statistic—but his parents... they'd have to live with it every single day for the rest of their lives. How do you get over that kind of failure?" Once he started, he couldn't stop. He let it all out until he was hunched over in his chair, blubbing like an idiot.

Sergeant Oda remained stoic, patting Sasaki's back, simply listening until he was done. "Sorry, sir," Sasaki said after a long pause, his head lowered and cheeks even redder than before.

He expected to be reprimanded. It's what his old man used to do. *Don't be such a wimp. Boys don't cry. Just man up and deal with it!* That lesson had been beaten into him on a daily basis. All he could do was apologise and teach himself not to cry in public. Not the kind of habit you just outgrow.

A warm hand on his head ruffled his hair, like you would to comfort a child. "Nothing to apologise for."

When they first met, Sasaki had thought Sergeant Oda was an ogre—hard, unfeeling, and intimidating as hell. But now he could tell that he was one of the few truly kind-hearted people in the world, constantly looking out for other people, putting them before himself.

"Thank you, sir. I may be out of line saying this, but your daughter is really lucky to have a father like you."

Sergeant Oda's cheeks flushed, and he gave an awkward chuckle. "It's kind of you to say so. Come on, I think we could both do with a beer or two."

"What is this place, sir?" The *izakaya* was full of other off-duty policemen, some still in uniform and others in plain clothes, with their badges either pinned to their shirts or lying on the table in front of them. Three younger officers in the corner looked considerably more drunk than they ought to have been, even off-duty; and were singing horrendously off-key. Empty glasses covered the table with only a tiny bowl of *edamame* as an appetiser.

*Great idea. Drinking on an empty stomach...*

"Hey, Oda! Long time, no see." A man, similar in age to Sergeant Oda, called from the bar. He was sitting with a group of five other officers.

"Been a while, Tachibana. Congratulations on the new addition. How many is that now?" Sergeant Oda said while Sasaki stood off to the side.

He wasn't big on crowds. Or strangers.

"Three, if you can believe it. What about you and your wife? Your only kid's about to set off for university, isn't she? Perfect time to have another." The man winked at Sergeant Oda, and all Sasaki could think was that it was an awkward conversation to be having in front of a bunch of strangers.

"One's enough for us, thanks. I don't think you've met our newest officer at Urawa. This is Sasaki."

"A pleasure to meet you, sir," Sasaki said, bowing his head.

"Likewise. I'm Sergeant Tachibana from Kita-Urawa Police Station."

*Must be Sato's superior officer, then.*

"Almost everyone here's a cop, all from different districts. Minato here is from Ōmiya Station, Tanaka from Warabi Station, Ito from Toro Station, and Yamamoto from Asaka Station," Sergeant Oda said, introducing the men around the table, each bowing their head respectively.

"They all have bars in their own areas, of course, but it's nice to drink with people who understand the stresses of the job, you know what I mean?" Sergeant Tachibana said.

He was as gruff as he appeared; short hair, shaved around the bottom and sides, time-worn face, and angular bone structure. He looked like a stereotypical sergeant from an American war film. Sasaki drank his beer, guzzling it down in five seconds' flat.

"Whoa there, rough day?" Ito, a younger officer in his mid-thirties, asked. He'd gone through at least three beers himself, by the look of it.

"Rough couple of months..." Sasaki replied, signalling the bartender for another glass.

"I hear that. We've been putting in double time trying to find this missing girl," Sergeant Ito said, drinking another half-pint. "It's been crazy."

Sergeant Oda and Sasaki glanced at each other; eyebrows raised. "What missing girl?"

"Oh yeah, it's not your area, so you probably haven't heard yet. A little half-Japanese girl went missing near Toro Station about two months ago. Her dog too. They were out taking a walk and just disappeared. No witnesses, no suspects, no clues; making our job almost impossible."

"Must be something in the water. We've been looking into a missing kid in our district too," Sergeant Tachibana said, taking a deep drag of his cigarette. "A little boy."

Sergeant Oda put his drink down, staring out into space. Sasaki could practically hear the gears in his head turning.

Sergeant Oda stood, putting his fingers in his mouth to produce a loud whistle that cut through the chatter. "Show of hands—who's currently investigating a missing kid in their district?" he shouted, addressing every officer in the bar. "No witnesses, no suspects?"

Sasaki's stomach dropped as he scanned the room. Even a veteran like Sergeant Tachibana looked shaken as every other officer slowly raised their hand. Six stations in total, spanning from Warabi all the way to Toro and Niiza.

Sergeant Oda resumed his seat, slamming his fist on the counter until his knuckles turned red.

"He knew," he said through clenched teeth. "The bastard knew our stations aren't interconnected… That we wouldn't notice the connection if he only took one kid from each district. No witnesses, no clues. He's playing our system like a fucking violin."

The bar fell silent, the air thick with the horrifying implication that their city had become a serial kidnapper's personal playground.

# Connections

"SO, WHAT DO we know so far?" Sergeant Oda asked, poised with a pen and paper. All the men seemed quite out of place, huddled around Sergeant Oda's dining room table.

Sasaki took a deep breath. "We know that Daiichi Watanabe, age seven, was taken on his way home from school in Warabi on October 17th; somewhere between the school near Warabi Station and his home near Urawa Station."

"Good. What else?" Sergeant Tachibana asked.

"Well…" Sasaki rubbed the back of his neck. "His case almost went to you, Sergeant Tanaka, but was changed to us when it was thought he was taken closer to Urawa than Warabi; which we can now confirm, thanks to his teacher, Ms Saki's statement. She saw him leave at five p.m., so it's unlikely he was taken near the school. No witnesses. Sergeant Tanaka checked the security footage at Warabi Station and we checked at Urawa Station and found no one matching Daiichi's description. A dead end."

Probably not the best phrase he could have used.

"Not if I have anything to say about it," Sergeant Oda said, scribbling down the last details. He turned to Sergeant Ito. "Next."

Sergeant Ito nodded. "Next was Miyuki Tondo, also age seven, taken on November 15th. Of Japanese-Canadian descent, with sandy-blonde hair. We thought that would make her easier to track, but unfortunately not.

She was taken after school, not far from her home near Toro Station, along with the family dog, which she was taking for a walk. One eyewitness: A man who works at a TOBU convenience store across the way from the park. He saw her walking with our lead suspect: A 'foreign-looking' girl with copper hair, between the age of nineteen and twenty-five. But Miyuki was chatting happily with her, so the witness didn't think much of it at the time."

Sasaki sat bolt upright, slamming his hand on the table.

"Didn't Daiichi's teacher have copper hair?"

Sergeant Oda leaned back in his chair while biting the end of his pen. "She did. But she also has an alibi, confirmed by several witnesses."

"Damn…"

"Station workers at Toro didn't see her, or the dog. Although that's not surprising, since pets aren't allowed in.

So, no links between the two cases. We also checked the IP Cameras, and there was no sign of little Miyuki or a woman matching the witness's description."

Sasaki stood, then kicked the leg of his chair. "Damn it!"

"Easy there. My wife won't thank you for destroying her furniture," Sergeant Oda said, motioning for Sasaki to sit, so he did, taking deep, even breaths.

Sasaki wondered how he could remain so calm. "…Fine. Who's next?"

"If everyone's notes are correct, the next was Saya Yashida, age eight. Taken December 4th in Niiza Prefecture, also near her home." Sergeant Yamamoto stopped a moment, going pale before continuing. "The last victim, Akira Hamada, age eight, was also taken from Niiza, close to where Saya was taken, except he disappeared on March 6th."

"Possible connection?"

"I thought so at first, but while both kids were—*are*— the same age, they're different genders, took different routes to school, and are from different socioeconomic backgrounds. Besides, the lead suspect in Saya's case is a woman in her late twenties or early thirties in a business suit, black hair in a ponytail, and glasses. A divorce lawyer, according to witnesses. She even gave the neighbours her business card. Turned out to be bogus. But she *was* there. She *does* exist. We know that from the security footage at Higashi-Tokorozawa Station. We saw her and Saya get on the train," Sergeant Yamamoto continued.

"I feel like there's a 'but' coming," Sargent Oda mumbled.

"A big one." Sergeant Yamamoto sighed. "We didn't see them get off the train. Neither of them. They just disappeared."

Silence filled the room. "How is that even possible?" Sasaki asked after a long pause.

"That's the million-dollar question," Sergeant Tachibana replied, rubbing his temple. "I thought kids were meant to go home in groups?"

"They're supposed to, but not all do as they're told, apparently," Sergeant Oda replied.

"Do you really think this could all be the same person?" Sato asked tentatively.

"It can't be. None of the prime suspects even remotely resemble each other. The victims went to different schools, lived in different areas. I hate to say it, but I think you're grasping at straws here," Sergeant Tachibana said, hunched over with his arms crossed, irritable.

"You can say it. Doesn't mean it's true."

"You know we won't get paid overtime for this, right?" Sato chuckled, obviously trying to lighten the mood. Sasaki shook his head—Sato had always needed to learn to read the room. Guess he was still a slow learner.

Sergeant Tachibana glared daggers at the young officer.

"If you think that's more important than finding someone's missing kid, you'd better find yourself a new occupation, boy." Sato's cheeks burnt bright red. He seemed to shrink in his chair, suddenly so small, all trace of jovial confidence gone. He'd have to pick things up faster if he was going to make it with a mentor like Sergeant Tachibana.

"Shiho Masaoka, seven years old, was next. Went missing December 21st. Also taken on her way home from school, near Ōmiya Station," Sergeant Tachibana continued.

"Well, at least that's one connection."

"Sure, but it isn't much of one. Our key suspect is a twenty to thirty-year-old woman with medium-length light brown hair in a messy bun and an overall dishevelled appearance," Sergeant Minato replied.

Sergeant Ito scoffed. "Brilliant. That narrows it down to… almost every housewife in the district. Hardly matches the lawyer's description."

Sergeant Minato raised an eyebrow. "No shit. As you can imagine, we got more tips than we could handle."

No wonder his eyes were so tired, withdrawing deeper and deeper into their sockets by the second, it seemed. Sasaki hoped he didn't end up looking like that one day.

"Next?"

"Hideo Okumura, six years old, went missing on January 25th." Sato's voice cracked. "The youngest. His case isn't classed as a kidnapping. Well, not your typical one. When he didn't come home, his mother immediately called us, fearing his father had taken the boy with him overseas. She has full custody, you see. We're still trying to get in contact with his father to confirm the boy's whereabouts."

"How far did you get?"

"We know his father caught a plane to Singapore, but we

haven't been able to confirm if Hideo was with him," Sergeant Tachibana said, interrupting Sato before he could reply. He turned to Sato. "Might want to get a rush on that."

"Yes, sir." Sato's voice was low, almost a whisper.

"That means Akira was the last. So far." Sasaki sighed, his head pounding. A warm orange glow streamed in from the large living room window across from them.

Another day almost gone. Perhaps another child gone, too; yet to be discovered. Lost to the darkness. A painful lump formed in Sasaki's throat, making it hard to swallow.

Part of him wished he had never become a police officer. Another part of him felt ashamed for having such thoughts.

"Yes. Although there has been speculation that his parents might be at fault," Sergeant Yamamoto chimed in.

"How so?"

"According to his teacher, he often came to school with bruises or a limp. Some of his friends claimed he always had 'bug bites' on his arms. I'd wager they were actually cigarette burns. We learned from their neighbours that his father is an alcoholic and his mother a heavy smoker."

"You think the father killed him?" Sergeant Oda asked.

"It's possible. Even accidentally. But we found nothing suspicious on the property, and both were clearly upset about his disappearance, and I don't believe they were acting. We checked the security footage at Asaka Station and Niiza Station, but nothing came up. The film was corrupted."

"Corrupted?" Sasaki's brow furrowed.

"Yes. It cut out for several minutes at five p.m. at Niiza

Station. Not uncommon. The entire system can be buggy."

"Not that buggy, surely?" Sasaki asked, but only received a shrug in reply.

"So let me get this straight," Sergeant Tachibana said, sitting bolt upright, counting on his fingers.

"We have six cases, all in different districts, under different circumstances; different suspects all with different physical descriptions… and you think they're connected? I'm sorry, Oda, but you'll never convince any of our superiors to look into this further. Any similarities are circumstantial, at best."

Sergeant Oda slammed his fist on the table, making all the men jump. "Everything in *all* these cases is circumstantial at best!" He uncurled his bone-white knuckles and fingers, relaxed his shoulders, and lowered his voice. "We can't just do nothing."

Sergeant Tachibana rose from his chair, placing a hand on Sergeant Oda's shoulder, pausing a moment. "You've got to resign yourself to the fact that sometimes there's just nothing we can do." Eyes downcast, he waved goodbye before making his way to the entry. "Oh! Sorry, Sayoko," he said with an embarrassed chortle. "Almost crashed straight into you."

A light, feminine giggle followed, somehow bringing Ms Saki to mind. A soft pattering of footsteps on hardwood floors, and Sergeant Oda's daughter appeared from the entry. She bowed in the direction of the door, bidding Sergeant Tachibana goodbye.

"Welcome home, Sayoko," Sergeant Oda said with the most gentle expression Sasaki had ever seen on him. "Sorry, we had hoped to have this all done by the time you and your mother got home."

Sayoko waved her hand in dismissal, hiding behind a bashful smile. Her school satchel dangled in the other hand, looking far heavier than it ought to. "It's okay. I always study in my room, anyway. Is it going well?" she asked.

Sergeant Oda shrugged, his voice rising several octaves. "Could be better." An obvious understatement. "But don't you worry, we'll manage."

"You always do," she said, swiping a juicy red apple from the fruit bowl on the counter beside them. Perfect teeth pierced the unsuspecting flesh with a crisp crunch. Sasaki couldn't help but stare, even though he knew he shouldn't.

Suddenly, Sayoko's eyes locked onto his.

His palms started to sweat, but not from his previous immature giddiness. Something about this girl's eyes unsettled him. It was how he imagined one would feel when confronted with a snake or shark—freezing, too afraid to move or breathe or make a single sound.

Sayoko smiled sweetly at him, swallowing her mouthful of apple. "You must be Officer Sasaki. I hope my dad's not being too hard on you." She laughed that same light, airy laugh from before—the kind of laugh that effortlessly puts people at ease.

Sasaki could breathe again. He inclined his head, in somewhat of a daze. "It's a pleasure to finally meet you."

"Likewise," she replied, spinning on her heels and making her way to the stairs.

"Don't work yourself too hard," Sergeant Oda told her, his eyebrows drawn together with concern. Sayoko's smile sent a chill up Sasaki's spine.

"Don't worry, I won't."

# LOST, BUT NOW FOUND

HISAKO STARED AT Mochi's empty bed. She couldn't concentrate. Her life seemed to revolve around studying now. It felt like it'd been forever since she'd done anything fun. It had been weeks since she'd seen Sayoko. They hadn't met up even once over winter vacation. *I guess this is what it'll be like when we're at different universities...*

Hisako threw down her pen and sighed, staring at the picture of her and Sayoko on their class trip to Kyoto, displayed in a cute decorative frame at the edge of her desk.

They were standing on the balcony at Kiyomizu Temple, holding their hands out in a peace sign with wide smiles on their faces. *It really was the best view, though,* Hisako reminisced. *How does that saying go again? 'Do something like you're going to jump off the Kiyomizu stage,'*

Hisako thought, picking up the picture and tracing her finger along the embossed pattern on the frame.

*Pretty graphic for a proverb. You'd totally die if you jumped from all the way up there.*

She gently put the picture back in its proper place. Hisako's shoulders deflated as she thought of how that proverb fit Sayoko perfectly: She gave her all to everything she did, no matter what. Like she would be doing now: studying and reaching for the stars to achieve her dream.

*She'll work herself to death if she doesn't have someone to keep an eye on her.* Hisako looked at the clock. Four thirty.

She leapt off her chair and picked up her shoulder bag, clambering down the stairs. "I'm going out!" she called, looking around. "Mom?"

"She's out shopping." Hisako hadn't seen Satoru hunched over on the sofa, playing his Nintendo DS.

"Okay. Can you tell her when she gets back? I'll be at Sayoko's," she said, patting her little brother's head.

He swatted her away like an annoying fly, not taking his eyes off his game. He was mature for a seven-year-old, but he was still just a kid. "I will. Say hi to Saya for me."

Hisako's plastic shopping bags swung from side to side, hitting her legs when she left the 7-Eleven. Some elementary school kids bumped into her—they'd been laughing and fooling around while they walked—and offered a quick sorry before running off.

Their yellow school hats were bright in the late-afternoon sun. *I guess there are still a lot of schools that have classes every Saturday. Thank God we don't*, Hisako thought.

She opened her flip phone and quickly punched in a text message as she neared Sayoko's house.

Hey Sayoko, ~! (๑>◡<๑) I'm just heading to your house now.
I have your favourite snacks~ ♥ (•ω−) ~ ☆

Kids were yahoo-ing over at Yono Park. Hisako couldn't help but smile, remembering all the fun she and Sayoko used to have playing there; even Satoru, when he was a toddler. They used to push him around in their toy pram, (under Hisako's mom's strict supervision, of course.)

*I wonder if we traumatised him. He hasn't been back here in ages*, Hisako thought. She rang the doorbell. *I should bring him and his friends here sometime.*

"Oh, hi, Hisako, what a surprise!"

"Hi, Mrs Oda. Is Sayoko home? I thought she could use a study buddy." Hisako held up her bag of goodies.

"How lovely. But I'm afraid she's not home yet. She said she was going to look in at Saitama Medical University Moroyama on the way home from the library, so I'm not sure when she'll be back. Why don't you come wait inside? We have the air-con on," Mrs Oda said in a sing-song voice, waving her hand and ushering Hisako inside.

"I sent her a text to let her know I was coming," Hisako said, heading to the kitchen and opening the freezer door, placing four pottles of Super Cup ice cream inside. Two melon flavour, one vanilla, and one chocolate. Sayoko and her dad were both crazy for anything melon flavoured.

“Thank you, dear. That’s so thoughtful of you. Go right ahead. I’ll turn on the a/c in Sayoko’s room, if you want to study in there while you wait.”

That was an offer Hisako took gladly.

She bounded up the stairs to Sayoko’s room. It hadn’t changed a bit. There were still bugs on display all over the walls and a gigantic pile of manga and light novels by her bed. One volume was upside down, with the pages splayed out right next to Sayoko’s pillow.

*Glad to see she’s been reading the manga I recommended.* Hisako picked up the book and skimmed its pages. *She’s almost up to the good part.* She put the book back, being extra careful not to lose Sayoko’s place, and chose a different manga to read while she waited.

After about twenty minutes, Hisako’s phone started playing the theme song from Sailor Moon. It was a text from Sayoko.

> Sorry ~! ||| ( °Δ° ) ||| I’m just catching my last train from Moroyama. I should be back soon ( ´ ▽ ` ).｡ｏ ❤

*At least she doesn’t sound like she’s stressing too much,* Hisako thought. She took her book over to Sayoko’s desk—she’d be able to see when Sayoko came home through the window that way. On her desk, right next to a jar of silver pins, was the same picture of them at Kiyomizu Temple.

It had been mounted in a larger frame with some print club pictures she and Hisako had taken at an arcade a while ago; pulling funny faces, holding their hands together to make the shape of a love-heart, with 'best friends forever' written in fluorescent font at the bottom of the last picture.

*That was so much fun. We should go again after we graduate.* The thought of going their separate ways made Hisako's chest feel tight. She knew they'd always be friends, but they'd hardly ever been apart since they were little.

She'd miss her. Nothing would be the same.

"Hisako, dear, would you like some iced barley tea?" Mrs Oda called from downstairs, making Hisako jump and bang her knee on the bottom of the desk, sending half of its contents flying.

"Ow! Yes, please. Thanks," she called back, rubbing her knee. All the pins had fallen out of the jar and Sayoko's small, rectangular jewellery box had popped open, spilling everything all over the floor. Hisako crouched down to pick everything up, scouring the carpet for any earrings that might have fallen out while she put the bigger things back— necklaces, rings, and the odd hair clip.

"Ooh, this is cute," she said, thinking aloud while she examined the hair clip. It was shaped like a cherry blossom, made from soft-textured oriental fabric, like what you get in Kyoto. Hisako saw something else out of the corner of her eye, by the bed. Something blue and sparkly.

She thought it was a bracelet, but when she picked it up,

she recognised it. A baby-blue leather collar with white rhinestones and an engraved, heart-shaped silver tag dangling from the middle: MOCHI.

She couldn't move. She tried to breathe, but it just kept catching in her chest. Hisako remembered Mochi leaving out her window the last day she saw him—he was definitely wearing it. She never took it off him.

Dark red crusted the rhinestones and clasp, too dark to be rust. More like blood.

*If Sayoko had found it somewhere, she would have told me, wouldn't she? I don't understand...*

She held the collar to her chest, trying not to cry as she rocked backwards and forwards. "She knows how much Mochi means to me. If she knew something, anything, about him, she'd tell me..." she told herself, her voice soft as a whisper. "If he was hit by a car or if she found him on the side of the road, she would've told me... she would have... so at least I would know what happened to him." A horrible feeling came over her as the voice inside her head told her she was wrong.

Hisako nearly crashed into Mrs Oda on her way down the stairs. "Oh! I was just about to bring you your tea," Mrs Oda said. "Are you alright? You look pale."

"I-I'm suddenly not feeling so good. I think I'll just head home," Hisako said, faking a smile and practically running out the door; the collar weighing heavily in her skirt pocket.

# RESTRICTED AREA

HISAKO HID HERSELF behind a tree just outside the school gate, waiting for Sayoko to pass by.

Almost two weeks had passed since she'd found Mochi's collar, and still nothing from Sayoko. Not even a hint that she might know what had happened to him. She was acting totally normal.

Sayoko had already texted Hisako earlier that she couldn't walk home with her again today; that she'd borrowed her dad's train pass so she could take the bullet train to Kyoto University, since it was a half day. Before, all of Sayoko's spontaneous commutes made sense, but now they just seemed suspicious.

Hisako kept Mochi's collar tucked away in her pocket, like a talisman.

Sayoko finally came out of the school gate, having changed out of her uniform and carrying a white tote bag. Hisako followed her, trailing behind, out of sight. She got strange looks from people passing, but she didn't care.

Sayoko took a shortcut through Yono Park, smiling and greeting parents watching their kids; she even stopped to give a little girl a push on the swing.

*I don't understand. She's always so friendly. Satoru adores her,* Hisako thought, her stomach twisting into knots. Retrieving Mochi's collar from her pocket, she squeezed it to remind herself that it wasn't just her imagination. Something didn't add up. She steeled herself then pressed on, shadowing Sayoko past the bakery, then the Kacchan Ramen shop, until they finally reached Yono-Hommachi Station. Sayoko went straight to the machine and bought her ticket before proceeding through the wicket.

*That's weird,* Hisako thought, scanning her Suica IC card to get through to the platform. *Why didn't she use her IC card?* They'd taken the train together thousands of times in the five years since the card system had been implemented, and Hisako had never seen Sayoko buy a physical ticket. Not once. They were too much of a pain when calculating transfers.

Hisako hid herself behind one of the massive, tiled pillars on the opposite side of the platform. Sayoko waited behind the yellow line, reading her book.

The train station was unusually quiet, with only a few other commuters waiting.

まもなく、埼京線に大宮駅方面行きがまいります。

*The train bound for Ōmiya Station on the Saikyo Line will arrive momentarily.*

危ないですから黄色い線までお下がりください。

*Please wait behind the yellow line.*

Hisako followed Sayoko onto the train, getting into the next car so she could still see her through the window.

Sayoko kept her head down, reading her book the entire way, making the occasional note in the margin with the pencil tucked behind her ear.

*Just looks like she's studying, no surprises there...*

次は大宮。大宮。お出口は右側です。

*Next stop, Ōmiya Station. Ōmiya Station. Doors will open on the right-hand side.*

Sayoko snapped her book shut and rushed off the train. Hisako trailed after her, weaving through the crowd and stopping at the odd vendor to pretend to shop when it seemed like Sayoko was going to turn around and catch her. Sayoko made a sharp left in the opposite direction of the *shinkansen* platform bound for Kyoto.

*Where's she going?* Hisako felt like a lioness stalking its prey. Ōmiya Station was way more crowded than Yono Station, and now that Sayoko was out of her uniform, she blended in better with the masses of people. Hisako was almost too scared to blink in case she lost sight of her. No one gave either Hisako or Sayoko a second glance. They were too absorbed with what they were doing and where they were going.

"Excuse me, pardon me," Hisako mumbled as she worked her way through the horde, not taking her eyes off Sayoko. She saw her move towards the restrooms by the East Exit, then nothing. She was gone.

Hisako stopped and looked around, waiting for Sayoko to resurface, but she didn't. When Hisako went over to the restrooms, she noticed the doors were a different colour to the one she saw Sayoko go through.

*It was more wooden*, she thought, her heart beating with the adrenaline. She couldn't have just disappeared.

Hisako went up on her tiptoes, stretching to get a better look through the crowd, but slipped on the freshly polished floors and plummeted to the ground. She groaned, rubbing her grazed elbow, and swore under her breath.

That's when she saw it—a concealed alcove behind the restrooms. She moved her head left to right, noting how it was only visible from the left angle. It was boarded off with plywood, the exact colour of the door she'd seen Sayoko go through. The words "RESTRICTED AREA" were written in red spray paint. Sheets of plywood were nailed on top of each other, with only one neat rectangular section off to the side. It was longer than it was wide: the perfect shape for a door. *But how do you get in?* Hisako thought, gliding her hands over it and pushing lightly on the corners. It gave way and popped open about one centimetre, easily opening the rest of the way, just wide enough for a person to squeeze through. Hisako glanced at the small white gadget mounted on the sideboard and the back of the door.

*Looks just like what we have on our handle-less kitchen cupboards.* She crept through the opening, spotting a tiny handle screwed on the inside of the door so she could pull it shut behind her. The sound of trains echoed from above, and it would've been pitch black if not for the whirring, flashing ceiling lights. The dank, musty smell was so overpowering, Hisako could almost taste it.

*Who knew all this was down here? Looks like an old, abandoned train platform...* Half of the tiles covering the large square pillars had fallen down and smashed, and the bumpy tiles to guide the blind looked more khaki green than their original bright yellow. Large oil stains pooled along the floor, some patches wet, others dry and caked on. Hisako hopped around them, trying not to get any on her shoes.

She couldn't see Sayoko anywhere but stayed in the shadows, just to be safe. There was a sheet of plywood propped up on two boxes in the centre of the platform, where the light was strongest.

Hisako crept out of the darkness to investigate.

The impromptu table was laid out like a study desk, with papers, books, pens, and tools scattered about. A cherry-shaped pottle of TonyMoly lip balm was near the front edge of the desk, next to a mortar and pestle, a sheet of paper covered with white residue, and a half-empty sheet of pills. The tablets must have been crushed and put into the empty lip balm pot. Hisako checked the back of the plastic sheet.

*Rohypnol...?*

Several stacks of medical books and journals with stamp marks from different libraries, like Saitama Central Library, Saitama Nanasato Library, and Sakuragi Library, were piled up around the workspace.

*She wouldn't have needed to go to any of these places... the Ōmiya Library around the corner would have had copies of all these books.* Hisako put the books back exactly where she found them, then turned her attention to a large, overstuffed notebook in prime position at the centre of the desk, beside an old polaroid camera. She instantly recognised Sayoko's delicate handwriting, neatly written on every page.

A lump formed in her throat and a shiver went down her spine as she read through its contents. She soon realised that she had never known her friend at all.

# DEAR DIARY

### Experiment #1

Feline. White Persian        September 20th, 2010
Notable Features: Blue collar. White fur.
Overweight.

Case Notes: Subject willingly volunteered,
entering through my bedroom window. Duct
tape proved sufficient to silen—

The diary fell to the platform floor and a small, strangled cry escaped Hisako's lips as she tried to stifle a scream. She had thought that knowing what had happened to Mochi would give her closure. Wrong.

Hisako hurled the diary across the platform, hitting one

of the thick, square pillars. Hisako closed her eyes. She couldn't continue. She just… couldn't. Not about Mochi. Not about her closest companion since her dad had died.

Sobbing, she went over to the pillar and picked up the diary, knowing she had to keep reading. Tears trickled down her cheeks as she turned to the next page.

## Subject #1

Human. 7 Year old male.
October 17th, 2010

Notable Features: 3 missing teeth. Black hair. Brown eyes. Average height and build for age. Outwardly healthy.

Case Notes:
Subject initially took well to the sedation (Rohypnol, as proper surgical anaesthetics are currently unattainable).
Removal of outer dermis was interesting: far more difficult to cut through than expected.
Considerable amount of pressure on the scalpel was required. Once removed, inspection of the muscle and tendons of the left arm and right leg was possible, and quite enlightening. Removal of the eyelid without scratching or damaging the eyeball was difficult, but achievable.

I'm certain I can do better next time.
Perhaps removing the eye first with a spoon?
Concluded that the subject has acute otitis media in left ear (ear infection). Closer inspection possible after amputation of the outer ear. Eardrum was swelled, bulging out differently from the healthy ear.
I cut it open and an influx of pus and fluid oozed out. A nasty infection indeed.
Should have been on antibiotics.
Examining the optic nerves proved challenging, as the subject woke up during examination.

Note to self: adjust to higher dose of sedation for future subjects. I had wanted to learn from a living specimen, but, alas, subject expired after only a few minutes of awakening.
I can only surmise that the subject died of shock. Oh well. How does that saying go?
"If at first you don't succeed, try and try again."

## Subject #2

Human. 7 Year old female.
October 26th, 2010

Notable Features: Mixed race. Blonde hair. Average build. No scars or birthmarks.

Arrived with white dog, breed: Shiba Inu.

Case Notes:
Dose of Rohypnol for sedation increased. Much more successful. As was pacification of the dog by mixing steak juice into my hand moisturiser. Working on a canine subject was fascinating, but not much practical use.
Really only any good for dismembering and practising sutures. Oh well.

The human subject proved more enlightening. I continued from where I left off on Subject #1, having a second attempt at cleanly removing the eyelid after removing eyeball with a spoon. Also more successful. One might even say perfect.
Already significantly more experience than the average applicant. The professors at Tokyo U, I'm sure, would be proud of my efforts.
Proceeded with preserving the eyeball in an airtight jar to allow for careful dissection at a later date.

Subject still successfully sedated and, most importantly, still alive. Deciding to be bold, I attempted my first proper amputation.
An ear is too simple. Only cartilage, no bone. Fingers seemed like a good place to start.

Ensuring to wear protective eye-wear and a mask, I used the saw I'd already purchased from DCM Homac, and I must say, it worked brilliantly to cut through the small bones. Not much I could do about the blood loss without the proper machinery, so I had to work quickly. File the bones into soft rounds so it wouldn't pierce the flesh, then neatly take the fragile flaps of muscle, tendons, and skin and sew the wound shut.

I managed four whole fingers. By the last one, my sutures drastically improved.

The first ones are a bit of an eyesore, but no matter. Practice makes perfect.

With such success, I felt confident enough to try a tonsillectomy. Much harder than I had anticipated. Started off strong, but couldn't get them to stop bleeding.

The subject expired. Which was disappointing, to say the least.

I should have waited on the tonsillectomy.

I'd have much preferred to try out my rib spreader and observe working organs.

No matter. I'll try it next time.

First mode of business, though, is to find the best way to cover the smell of decomposition...

# Subject #3

Human. 8 Year old female.
December 4th, 2010

Notable Features: Dark brown hair. Slightly overweight. Short for her age.

Case Notes:

Made an incision in abdomen to examine the different layers of muscle and fat deposits. I don't mind admitting that I was surprised by the colour and texture. Different from cutting through a finger or an ear. Easing the scalpel through the fat was much like the gooey texture found on raw chicken, except yellow. I had read about it and seen pictures in textbooks, but it's nothing like cutting through real, live flesh and muscle.

Content with my discovery, I carefully sutured each layer and exceeded my own expectations. But just as I finished stitching the final layer, the subject woke up, again. Damn it.

At least it didn't expire like the last one. Although, I was not pleased at having to bash such a precious commodity on the head so it'd stop thrashing.

For now, subject has been dosed with a fresh lot of sedative, to keep her quiet.

And duct tape over the mouth, just in case.

I should have been more careful. Tied her to a chair, or something, to keep her propped up. Arrived this morning to find subject lying on her back, choked to death on her own vomit.

Without the proper equipment, an autopsy provided little insight into cause of death, but seems as if the subject went into severe shock, potentially inducing a heart attack, which caused the vomiting. Or possibly an overdose. Now that I think about it, I had been in such a panic, I forgot to check the dosage. A stupid mistake I won't make again. So, no living organs to examine. Small kidney stones remained in the kidney. I can only assume either from a high salt diet, or perhaps subject was chronically dehydrated.

I've found that dismemberment works in my best interest for disposal. Then I can apply different experiments to see how particular environments and chemicals affect decomposition and odour. There's nothing more exciting than awaiting the results of an experiment. I feel all jittery just thinking about it.

# Subject #4

Human. 7 Year old female.
December 21st, 2010

Notable Features: Black hair. Underweight. Slightly below average height. Wrist in splint.

Case Notes:

An overall healthy subject, slightly underweight. Took well to the sedation. Wrist was in a splint, so peeled back the tissue and muscle to inspect for damage: a buckle fracture, based on my examination of the bone.

Given subject's smaller frame and injury, it is safe to assume subject plays some kind of sport. A dancer, maybe?

My rib spreader finally arrived, so seemed like the perfect opportunity to test it out and get a good look at fully operational internal organs. Not for very long, however. The subject's heart failed mere minutes after being opened up. It seems I'll not be able to accomplish such a feat until my second year of residency.

It'll be winter vacation soon. No school means no commute, and no commute means no more new subjects for a while.

I'll have to make this one last.

Removed the kidney, liver, intestines, and stomach. Perhaps I can preserve them with salt so they'll keep over the two-week vacation? Yes, I think I'll do that.

Then I can take my time to study each organ. What fun!

In other news, the results are in on the best method of disposal: limestone and an airtight environment. It smells so much better in here now, I'm glad to say.

It makes me want to come here more often.

## Subject #5

Human. 6 year old male.
January 23rd, 2011

Notable Features: Short black hair, brown eyes. Speaks with a lisp.

Case Notes:

This one did not go at all to plan. I don't know what happened. I made a tiny incision in the chest—the tiniest of tiny cuts. Minuscule. Yet it bled as if I'd severed an artery. I stitched the wound, applied natural anticoagulants, but nothing would stem the flow. Subject expired from blood loss.

So disappointing. I'll have to settle for

postmortem practice again.

Luckily, I made an exciting purchase of an E-valve jigsaw at DCM Homac just the other day, so I can proceed with trialling a new technique. A small consolation, but it will have to suffice.

The jigsaw proved effective for removing the crown of the skull to remove the brain for dissection. As learned from past errors, this time I ensured I wore a proper mask with filtered respirator so as not to breathe in any bone dust.

Health and safety first.

After further reading, I have come to the only logical conclusion that the bleeding was not my fault. It couldn't have been.

My form was perfect.

The subject, male, must have had a blood disorder, like haemophilia.

I did nothing wrong. What a relief.

## Subject #6

Human. 8 Year old male.
March 6th, 2011

Notable Features: Short black hair, dark brown eyes. Bruises along the ribs, arms, and cigarette burns on each forearm and collarbone.

Case Notes:
Why does everything have to be so difficult? Underlying conditions are fascinating, and great for experience, but they just make everything... messier.
I used the correct amount of sedation, I'm sure. And yet, after a perfect amputation (if I do say so, myself) of the left leg, halfway through suturing the skin flaps to neatly cover the bone, the subject regained consciousness. I'd kill for a proper anaesthesiologist. But all that will have to wait. As it happens, the subject suffered from severe asthma. Just my luck.
Cause of death: an acute asthma attack.
I suppose, at least, now I'll be able to compare his lungs with the healthy lungs of Subject #5.

Hisako threw the diary onto the floor, kicking it away as if it were poisoned.

Each diary entry had pages covered with polaroid photos of each child and what Sayoko had done to them: cheeks missing, teeth and muscle exposed, fingers removed and stitched back on, eyeballs torn from their sockets, noses cut off. Hisako counted six children in total.

Her nose ran and eyes watered, as if her emotions couldn't be contained, leaking out. Her hands trembled as she held them over her mouth and sobbed, Mochi's collar looped around her right hand.

Hisako hugged her knees to her chest; the back of her throat burned with bile and it took all her strength not to puke. Breathing was a chore. The room seemed to close in around her; the darkness and stagnant air enveloping her, overwhelming her senses.

Just when Hisako thought she was about to pass out, she noticed a lone note—a shred of paper—had slipped from the diary.

*Bring Hisako some leek soup or rice porridge tomorrow to make her feel better. Then I'll get to see Satoru, too. Kill two birds with one stone.*

# BEST FRIENDS FOREVER

A CLANGING SOUND echoed throughout the chamber, reminding Hisako that she hadn't seen Sayoko since she had snuck into the secret lab.

Hisako picked up the diary and loose pages and put them back where she found them on the desk. Then she clambered under the desk and squeezed herself into a ball, tucking her legs up to her chest.

There was a tapping of footsteps and the rustling of a full plastic bag being thrown off the platform onto the tracks. Hisako tried not to imagine what was inside. Sayoko softly hummed to herself—loud enough for Hisako to know that she was right behind her. Thank god the desk had a back. Sayoko's footsteps became quieter and quieter, followed by the creak of a door hinge and the closing of the push-catch. Hisako waited a few moments before peeking out of her hiding place. A quick glance confirmed Sayoko was gone.

*What if she comes back? I have to tell someone. Will they believe me? Mr Oda, he'll believe me. Have to get to Urawa...* Hisako crawled out from under the desk, but the platform was slippery from water dripping from the ceiling. She slipped and fell over the edge, landing on the tracks. She tried to sit up, but only sank further into the squishy pile of plastic bags, filled to bursting point. Brown-black sludge and dirt covered Hisako's skirt. Her face screwed up in revulsion. One bag split open under Hisako's weight, spilling its contents all over the tracks. She could almost taste the rotting meat; the crunching of tiny bones and the slimy texture of decaying flesh against her skin made her stomach lurch.

She didn't even try to stifle her screams this time.

She scrambled up and backed away, madly wiping herself off before collapsing against the side of the platform.

A small, once pink shoe toppled out of one of the bags; the little foot still inside. Swarms of rats scurried around the bags of little bodies, all eager to get a bite. A face stared back at Hisako from another bag, so badly decayed that she couldn't tell whether it was a boy or a girl. Although only black, empty sockets remained, its eyes seemed wide; terrified and haunting. Its open mouth screamed at her; It had three teeth missing. All Hisako could manage were choked, strangulated sobs.

*Then I'll get to see Satoru too.*
*Kill two birds with one stone.*

Hisako's heart sank. "Satoru." Hisako bolted, climbing up onto the platform and sprinting to the door without looking back. She thrust the door open and burst through, startling several people as she charged through the station.

*If she's going back to Yono, she'll have to take the Keihin-Tōhoku Line.*

"Hey, slow down!" one of the station workers yelled as Hisako spun on her heels and charged down the stairs onto the Keihin-Tōhoku Line platform, blending in with the crowd. Sayoko stood behind the yellow line on the left-hand side of the platform, reading a book.

Hisako inched closer, slowly nudging past people with her shoulder and elbows as she tried to get closer without alerting Sayoko. The ascending xylophone scale chimed over the loudspeaker.

まもなく、京浜東北線に与野駅方面行きがまいります。

The train bound for Yono Station on the Keihin-Tōhoku Line

will arrive momentarily.

危ないですから黄色い線までお下がりください。

Please wait behind the yellow line.

The rattling of an oncoming train filled the tunnel, followed by the deafening honking of a horn. Without hesitation, Hisako firmly grabbed Sayoko's shoulders. Sayoko arched her neck, looking behind her, her eyes wide and forehead creased. "Hisako?"

Hisako screeched, shoving Sayoko forward and sending her flying off the platform and onto the tracks. Sayoko lay stunned in the direct path of the oncoming train, her ankle bent at an odd angle, the bone threatening to peek through the skin. Her glasses lay at the opposite side of the tracks, the lenses cracked in several places. Onlookers held Hisako back while station workers scrambled for the emergency stop button. The brakes screamed along the tracks.

The bright light of the train's headlights flooded the station. Tears streamed down Hisako's cheeks as she saw Sayoko, her best friend, screaming for help and clawing at the ground, trying to drag herself to safety as the train sped towards her.

# Devastation

"SASAKI SPEAKING."

"It's Oda. I need you to go on ahead of me to Ōmiya Station. I'm just finishing up with a suspect, but I shouldn't be too long. Apparently there's been an accident, police presence required. The Ōmiya Police Station has requested our assistance, so it must be serious."

"Understood, sir." Sasaki hesitated. "A 'human accident' sir?" 'Human accident' was the euphemism station workers used for suicides by train. He'd learnt that the hard way.

"Not by the sound of it. Pushed, according to witnesses. It's not going to be pretty."

Sasaki grabbed his coat, buttoning it all the way to cover the coffee stain on his shirt, and hailed a taxi. It would be faster; the trains would be in for one hell of a delay.

*Fuck me... I knew today was going to suck.*

The scene crawled with police and station workers; the tracks cordoned off with yellow tape while they removed the body. It was the most devastating train accident Sasaki had ever seen. Blood plastered the wall and the front of the train itself. At least a dozen people were on the tracks trying to de-tangle the body.

A young man in a JR uniform was curled into a ball at the side of the platform, pale and obviously in shock. An older JR employee sat beside him, trying to console him.

*Must be the driver, the poor bastard...* Sasaki hesitated before going over to the tracks to see the body.

Sergeant Oda had been right: It wasn't a pretty sight. The girl's body, face down, had been torn clean in half, her upper body reaching out towards the platform, her internal organs spilling out behind her. Her fingers were bloody and mangled. Some of her nails had torn off when she tried to claw her way to safety. The train had dragged away her lower body when it reversed, her severed spine becoming entangled in the wheels and spokes under the train. It would take some time to remove it.

*Good God, she would've seen it coming.* A fizzing sensation formed in Sasaki's stomach. He tried not to puke, not wanting to add to the to the collection of vomit at the edge of the platform. He turned to the station workers, his hand covering his mouth. "Did anyone see what happened?"

"Christ, who *didn't* see it..." the older man scoffed, his hands shaking when he lit his cigarette. "Fifteen years I've worked here and seen nothing like it. Just pushed the kid right out in front of the train. There wasn't even enough time for the emergency brakes to kick in. We had to reverse the goddamned train just to get to her."

"And *her*?" Sasaki asked, nodding towards a pillar where a girl with dark brown hair in handcuffs sat, guarded by two station officers.

"The one who pushed her."

Sasaki made notes in his pocket notebook, his scribblings looking more like chicken scratches in his haste.

*She only looks like she's in high school.* "Did she say why?"

"Nope. Said she won't talk to anyone but the police, then clammed right up."

Sasaki glanced back at the girl. Brown muck covered her from head to toe, along with what seemed to be some form of dried blood. *There's more to this than she's letting on,* he thought, an eyebrow raised and eyes narrowed as he took the first few steps towards her.

"Sasaki."

Inspector Takeuchi waved to Sasaki, calling him away from the tracks. Sasaki stopped and saluted, straight-backed and with perfect posture. "Sir!"

"Is Oda with you?" Panic filled the Inspector's voice, and his sustained eye contact was unsettling.

Sasaki hesitated. "No, sir. I came on ahead."

"Good. I want you to get Oda as soon as he arrives and keep him as far away as possible."

The fizzing sensation intensified; his heart dropping to

his stomach. "Why, sir? Is something wrong?" Sasaki asked, his brows furrowed. Inspector Takeuchi lowered his gaze, his lips pressed together into a thin line. Sweat beaded his forehead and his hands were wringing nervously behind his back. A wave of panic washed over Sasaki. "Sir...?"

Inspector Takeuchi closed his eyes; his bottom lip trembling. "It's his daughter, Sayoko."

Sasaki's shoulders dropped, the world around him spinning. "What?"

"Sorry I'm late." Sasaki's heart stopped at the sound of Sergeant Oda's voice.

None of the Urawa officers could look him in the eye.

Sasaki rushed over to him, grabbing his shoulder and lightly pushing him back. "I th-I think you might want to sit this one out, sir," he stammered, clearing his throat as he fumbled over his words.

"Excuse me?" Sergeant Oda replied, his head cocked to the side, his mouth turned up in a confused smirk. Sergeant Oda tried to brush him aside, but Sasaki pushed back, harder this time.

"Please, sir..." Sasaki begged, knowing the fear in his voice was giving him away. "You really don't want to see this, sir." Sasaki could feel Inspector Takeuchi staring at him from the edge of the platform.

Sergeant Oda's smile slowly faded, his jaw slacked, and fear filled his eyes. Sasaki followed his line of sight—he was looking straight at the brown-haired girl in custody.

"Hisako?" Sergeant Oda said, his voice hoarse and

pupils contracted into pinpoints. Sasaki barely had the time to cry out as he was flung to the side, landing with a painful thud on his back from Sergeant Oda's judo throw. Sasaki and half the other officers screamed for him to stop, but Sergeant Oda charged over to the edge of the platform.

One glance. That's all it took.

Sergeant Oda collapsed, sinking to his knees, unable to support his own weight. "Sayoko!" he screamed.

Sasaki didn't know what to do as the resourceful, powerful, and formidable man he had come to respect broke down into anguished, incoherent sobs.

*There's no consoling this*, he thought, each heart-broken cry a dagger in his heart. Tears burned his eyes as he crouched down in front of Hisako. "Hisako, is it? I don't know who you are or how you're connected to all this, but why?" he asked, steeling his voice, surprised by how steady it was. "What could she possibly have done to deserve this?" Sasaki pointed towards the inconsolable Sergeant Oda. "What did *he* do to deserve this?"

"She deserved it." Neither Hisako's face nor voice held any trace of emotion. She was like a China doll, hollow and unfeeling.

"That's not an answer," Sasaki said.

Hisako simply stared at him, her haunted expression sending a chill up his spine. "Behind the East Exit restrooms. The alcove, behind the door."

# THE BLACK SMUDGE

SASAKI AND SERGEANTS Tachibana, Yamamoto, Tanaka, Minato, Ito, and Officer Sato gaped in silent horror at Sayoko's hidden lab. Now fully illuminated with floodlights and as many lamps as they could find, Sasaki had a full view of the 'lab', platform, and tracks.

The flashing of cameras blinded them, the irritating clicking of the shutters almost nonstop.

Sergeant Tachibana could only shake his head, taking the first step toward the first of the two makeshift desks. Sasaki followed. A polystyrene mannequin head sat to the far right, donning a black wig styled into a bob.

Sergeant Tachibana opened the bag next to it and pulled out wig after wig. Medium length copper with ringlets. A long, black wig, in a ponytail. Light brown, medium-length, in a dishevelled bun; and a short wig, cropped above the ears. He held it up for all the men to see, his eyes ablaze. An unpleasant feeling rose in Sasaki's gut and he was struck with the sudden urge to break something.

The table was strewn with fake nails adorned with cookie and bow embellishments, an impressive array of makeup in various shades and styles, colour contact lenses (if Sasaki remembered correctly, the kids nowadays called them 'circle lenses'), and sheets of pills.

A pile of clothes lay discarded on the floor: a woman's business suit, a floral white skirt, sweatpants, a shapeless t-shirt, and a high school baseball uniform. Beside it lay a neatly folded pile of children's clothing and an extra-large sports bag, the inside stained with dried blood and white fur and the red rim of a baseball cap peeking through the half open zipper.

*Daiichi...* Sasaki picked up one of the sheet of pills.

"Rohypnol, one milligram."

"That explains how the kids went so quietly," Sato said, trailing off as Sergeant Tachibana threw the wig to the ground, hard.

"No, it doesn't! How does she have so much of it? How did she get them to drink it? It turns bright fucking blue, for God's sake," he shouted.

Even the sergeants cowered before him.

Sasaki swallowed hard and turned to Sato. "Sato, find out who her doctor is—*was*—and get her medical record.

See who prescribed it, and for how long."

A moment's hesitation, then a nod. Sato left the lab, taking out his cellphone.

Sasaki dabbed a finger into the powder, staring at it. The container was small; small enough to fit into her pocket.

*But how ...* Sasaki gasped, electrified. "Cola."

"What?"

"She put it into a can or bottle of cola. Even if the bottle was transparent, the drink's almost black. You'd never notice it change colour." He grabbed the lip balm container and held it up. "If she had this in her pocket, she could easily slip it into a drink; especially if she offered to open it for them first. The kids would just think she was being nice. Even an adult wouldn't automatically assume their drink's been spiked right in front of the vending machine."

Sergeant Ito went pale. "A high school girl came up with that?"

Sasaki shrugged. "Why not? Her dad—" he paused, a pang of guilt shooting through his gut. "—her dad's a cop. She knows... *knew* how the system worked. Where the cracks are."

"Evil bitch," Sergeant Tachibana said, his face and neck flushing.

Sergeant Yamamoto picked up a cylinder, no bigger than a pen, from the table with his gloved hand. Sasaki puzzled for a moment. Sergeant Yamamoto clicked the button on the side, projecting a bright red dot onto the wall opposite the tracks. "A laser pointer," he said, dropping it into an evidence bag.

"Could that affect the station security cameras?" Sasaki asked. *Surely not. They only cost a couple of bucks.*

"Definitely," Sergeant Tachibana said. "This one's not just a cheap toy." Who'd have thought.

Sato came running back over to them, holding his hand over the receiver of his cellphone. "Her doctor prescribed the Rohypnol for insomnia," he said, in disbelief. "For months now. Because of stress over entrance exams, she told him. This was definitely premeditated, sir."

"Really? What was your first clue? The disguises, the tools? Or the entire fucking secret lab she built in the fucking subway?" Sergeant Tachibana snapped.

Sato's shoulders drooped and his gaze dropped to the floor as he inched further from Sergeant Tachibana, closer to the exit. He tentatively cleared his throat, his voice significantly quieter than before. "I've also confirmed that Hideo Okumura was, in fact, a haemophiliac and that Shiho Masaoka broke her wrist at ballet. So Sayoko's… well, 'case notes', were correct."

The men went silent as the coroner strolled past them, toward the tracks. Sasaki didn't want to see them. But he had to. Had to do a proper job. For Sergeant Oda and the children's families, if no one else.

The coroners, four in total, climbed down the ladder onto the tracks. Sasaki remained on the platform. A pile of garbage bags, just like Hisako had described, were on the right side of the tracks; some broken, spewing body parts and decomposing flesh. Fine white powder dusted the entire area, including inside the bags.

"What's that?" he asked.

The coroner shrugged. "Well, it's certainly not flour." Sasaki glared at him. "Could be limestone dust."

"Limestone? Why?" Sasaki turned away while men sorted through the body parts that had spilled over. His stomach lurched.

"Removes odours like you wouldn't believe. Probably the only reason this place doesn't stink to high heaven."

"Hey. Watch it. That 'stink' is somebody's children."

The coroner looked away, his movements slow and sheepish. "Sorry."

Sasaki turned his attention to the left of the tracks, where Sergeant Tachibana and the other sergeants were currently engrossed in examining some kind of makeshift rectangular enclosure. It had five compartments held up by wooden stakes, and each compartment was separated and contained with clear plastic held together with duct tape.

Sasaki couldn't quite make out what was inside.

"We found a roll of polyethylene film over there," Sergeant Tachibana said, motioning to the desks and 'surgery table.' Sasaki hesitated, not really wanting to know what it was for. His stomach lurched again.

He willed himself not to be sick, but when Sergeant Tachibana opened each compartment, one by one, there was no stopping it. *One way to use an XL evidence bag.*

All the men covered their noses as a rush of decay

spilled out, contaminating the surrounding air. Plastic film now removed, what lay sealed inside was abundantly clear.

The first compartment contained common garden soil as sediment, on top of which was what used to be a child's arm from the elbow down, including the hand.

The second compartment contained rocks and paving stones; also accompanied by small, mangled, decomposing body parts. Sasaki jerked away, dry heaving. Pain pricked his palms as he dug his fingernails in, his own pain a welcome distraction.

The coroner passed him a notebook, pages bulging, disgust marring his own face. "Here," he said, flipping the notebook open so Sasaki could see the exact contents he was referring to. Sasaki's brow furrowed.

All present fell silent as Sasaki read aloud.

"The thought occurred to me sometime in late November that if I am to continue my work here, unimpeded, I'd better test out the best form of body disposal. And while I'm at it, it wouldn't hurt to experiment how different environments affect decomposition. That has always fascinated me, and such knowledge would only benefit my studies…" Sasaki stopped a moment to compose himself and to will the tears blurring his vision to piss off. He inhaled deeply and continued with staggered breaths. "After all, 'No man's knowledge can go beyond his experience,' as John Locke said. And who can argue with that? If one had the choice of a well-read surgeon with exceptional theoretical knowledge or a surgeon with more experience in the operating theatre, they'll pick experience every time." Lip curled, Sasaki thrust the book into Sergeant Tachibana's hands. His desire to shoot someone was never as strong as in that exact moment. It was almost a shame she was already dead. She deserved worse.

Crouching and facing away from the enclosure, he could hear Sergeant Tachibana flipping through the pages, slowly, intently.

"This is how she knew to use limestone and air-tight garbage bags," he said dryly, snapping the book shut. "Not once does she refer to them in a way that's even remotely human. More like cadavers, even when they were alive."

Tears rolled down Sasaki's cheeks. Rocking on his heels, he prayed for the day to be over already so he could leave, although his heart ached at the thought that the children never would.

Day three, and Sasaki was still plagued by nightmares where he was alone in those dark, desolate tunnels with the mutilated bodies of the missing children clawing at him, screaming.

*Help us!*          *Please!*          *We want to go home...*

Tiny fingernails scraped at his arms and legs, rotting flesh sliding from muscle and bone. Open mouths with missing teeth and mutilated cheeks screamed and cried as they pulled him deeper, deeper into the tunnels, their dead eyes glowing red.

*Help us.*

He would wake up screaming, sheets and clothes drenched in sweat, dreading having to get up and go back.

Sasaki massaged the bridge of his nose, taking a sip from his third coffee of the morning.

Industrial lamps bathed the underground tunnel in cool light as the officers continued their work. Flashing cameras worsened Sasaki's threatening migraine.

The bodies had all been identified by their dental records or DNA, matched from tissue samples. The news that the arm from the first compartment belonged to little Hideo Okumura broke Sasaki's heart, but it was even more devastating to Sato. Sasaki had spent the early hours of that morning on the phone with Sato, trying to console him. Hideo's father had flown back to Japan upon hearing of his son's disappearance. Sato confided that once he informed him of his son's death, he couldn't get the sound of the man's anguished cries out of his head.

"They haunt me all night and all day. I can't sleep. I can't eat. Can't get that disgusting rotting smell out of my nose." He had started sobbing, then. "I don't know what to do," he had said, distraught. Neither did Sasaki.

So he had said nothing.

"You look as rough as I feel," Sergeant Tachibana said with the tiniest flicker of a smile. Surrounded by death, everyone lacked their usual spark.

Sasaki couldn't smile back. "Yeah, well… you know."

"Indeed, I do." Sergeant Tachibana placed a hand on Sasaki's shoulder, giving it a light squeeze. "Don't hold it all in. Or it'll eat you up inside until there's nothing left."

Sasaki couldn't even nod. Feelings overwhelmed him, and yet, he also couldn't feel anything at all. Numb.

He hesitated, then mumbled. "Perhaps you should have told Sato that."

"What?" Sergeant Tachibana asked, confused.

Sasaki said nothing. Maybe that had been the problem.

He should have told his friend that it was going to be alright; that they were in this together, that they'd get through this. But he hadn't. And now it was too late.

Sasaki opened and closed his mouth as he tried to find the words to tell Sergeant Tachibana that Sato had been found that morning, hanging from his ceiling fan.

"Wow, this is next level stuff." All the officers' heads turned to the sound of the voice: a young man in a pristine, tailored suit and flashy sunglasses.

"Can I help you?" Sasaki asked. He injected just the right amount of 'I don't have time for this shit' in his tone. The man passed Sasaki his business card, but pushed on without giving him enough time to read it. He removed his glasses and made a beeline to the 'surgery' table, peering over them with delight.

"Wow. I have this exact same woodworking saw set from DCM Homac! She used all this for *surgery*?" There was too much awe in his voice for Sasaki's liking.

Sergeant Tachibana's too, judging by his tone. "Who the hell let you in here? This is a crime scene. Get out, before I make you."

"I'm Kenjiro Ando—a criminal psychologist from Tokyo. Got straight on a train when I heard about all this. It's such a shame... I would have liked to study her alive. It's not every day you come across a psychopath of this magnitude. And so young, too. Is it true she managed to buy a rib spreader online and have it sent to a P.O. Box under a fake name using the money her parents gave her for train fare?" He laughed as if it were a big joke. "How embarrassing."

Something snapped inside Sasaki.

He seized the man by his collar and slammed him up against the wall.

"What the fuck is wrong with you? Eight people are dead, six of which are children, with another committed to a mental hospital, and all you're thinking about is what made her fucking tick?" Ando's lower lip trembled, his mouth hanging open as Sasaki lifted him higher off the ground. "She may have been an evil fucking monster, but she was still someone's daughter. And the last thing the Oda's need right now is an insensitive prick like you sniffing around and analysing every little thing they may or may not have done throughout Sayoko's life for her to turn out like that. And don't even get me fucking started on the families of the victims." Sasaki's eyes bore into the man's. "If I find out you've been harassing anyone, and I mean *anyone*, related to this case, I'll toss you into the deepest, darkest dungeon I can find and throw away the fucking key."

Ando stumbled as Sasaki shoved him back towards the door, straightening his collar before he left. The room burst into applause. It seemed Sasaki wasn't the only one who still respected Sergeant Oda.

"Excuse me, sir," a young man in a JR uniform called from the doorway, motioning for Sasaki to come over.

*Don't blame him for not wanting to come in here...*

The man bowed and passed Sasaki an external hard drive. "The IP Camera recordings from the day of the incident, sir. As requested."

"Right. Thank you."

Sasaki brought the recording back to Urawa Police Station to watch with the officers from Kita-Urawa, Ōmiya, Warabi, Toro, Asaka, and Niiza.

The office didn't feel the same without Sergeant Oda.

*He didn't have to resign... it wasn't his fault.* Sasaki plugged in the hard drive, projecting the video onto a larger screen, glancing at each of the men before pressing the 'play' button. "Ready?"

"Just get on with it," Sergeant Tachibana grumbled. None of them wanted to watch it, but it was still evidence. They had already agreed to drown themselves in booze at their favourite *izakaya* afterwards.

The image on the screen was in black and white and

clear as mud. Tilting his head, Sasaki said, "Uh, what am I looking at here?" to no one in particular. "This is supposed to be in high definition."

Sergeant Tachibana shrugged. "Probably corrupted."

"How?"

"Don't know, don't care. Keep playing."

Sasaki rested his chin on his hands. So far, everything was just as the witnesses described. There had been no doubt that Hisako had deliberately pushed Sayoko onto the tracks, but it was even more apparent on tape. The men all flinched when the train pulled into the station and blood spattered the walls and the witnesses standing at the edge of the platform. The recording skipped intermittently; people moving in broken lines rather than in a smooth motion. *Far from HD*, Sasaki thought. *But it should be...*

Suddenly, he removed his chin from his hands, jolting up at full attention, his mouth hanging open like a codfish.

"What was that?"

"What was what?" Sergeant Tachibana asked testily.

"That." Sasaki pointed to a large black smudge by the edge of the platform as it sped across the screen.

"A black smudge. To be expected with such shitty film quality."

Sasaki snatched the remote from the table, the images speeding back in time while he rewound and changed the speed setting, playing it back frame by frame.

The men leaned in, barely blinking as each still image became more terrifying than the last.

A dark, spectral shadow clawed its way up the platform, pulling itself up off the tracks; long hair cascading over its shoulder. Its fingers were three times as long as an average human's; the tips sharp points, like blades.

The lower body was gone.

Only shadowy entrails dragged behind it. Red, glowing eyes stared back at them, locking onto the camera before the figure dragged itself along the ground and scampered away at alarming speed, like a demonic spider.

They stared at the screen, then at one another. No one was willing to verbalise who or what they just saw.

# TEKETEKE

HISAKO TOSSED AND turned in her sleep, re-living the same nightmare she'd been having for months.

Every night was the same: She found herself lost in the train tunnels, stumbling blindly in the dark, feeling her way along the cold, wet walls as she searched for a way out.

The same sound followed her, getting louder and louder with each passing minute.

SCRIIIIIIIIITCH

SCRAAAAAAAATCH

It was all she could hear over the sound of her own heartbeat: the sound of bodies dragging along the ground.

She would wander the tunnels in an endless loop, occasionally feeling something cold grab at her ankles, the slimy flesh of the murdered children. A cat's scream cut through the darkness, followed by giggles. A strange substance hung from the ceiling, tickling her nose and face.

It smelt just like Sayoko's favourite melon-scented shampoo.

SCRIIIITCH

SCRAAATCH

Needles pricked at her legs, slogging their way up to her waist, arms, and shoulders. Red glowing eyes stared up at her as the creature climbed to her eye level, its fiery gaze burning her from the inside out.

Thick, wet blood and intestines oozed down Hisako's front from the creature's gaping wound; bone scratched her legs where the spine had been severed.

Hisako always woke up just as she was being torn in half by razor-sharp claws, long and pointed like the end of a scythe; while the children raked at her feet, groaning, begging for her to save them. Hisako awoke with a horrified screech, alerting the nurses on-call; her heartbeat dangerously fast.

"Easy there, it's okay, it's okay. Deep breaths—in—and out," an older nurse said, her voice steady while two orderlies held Hisako down. Hisako screamed and writhed under their weight, scratching and slapping at them. The scars on her wrists throbbed despite being fully healed.

She felt the prick of a needle in her arm and her head swam. "There we go, that's better, isn't it?" the nurse crooned, strapping Hisako's wrists and ankles to the four corners of the bed.

The door slamming and the lock being bolted in place sounded faraway, as if Hisako was listening to it while underwater. She groaned, her head lolling from side-to-side, the drugs calming her and making her woozy rather than knocking her out.

She tried to focus on the dripping washbasin tap, consistent and comforting; like counting sheep.

Drip.

*One sheep.*

Drip.

*Two sheep.* Her heartbeat started to steady with the sound of the drips.

Drip. Drip.

*Three she—*SCRIIIIIIITCH

SCRAAAAAAAATCH

Hisako's eyes snapped open. A black shadow in the far corner by the ceiling caught her eye, jerky and rapid as it climbed down, inching closer and closer to the bed. Hisako's chest bobbed uncontrollably as she took fast, shallow breaths through her nose.

*It's just a dream... It's just a dream...*

She twisted her hands around her restraints, willing them to snap so she could run away.

SCRIIITCH

SCRAAAATCH

The shadow came closer, claws screeching as they carved scratch marks into the floor; its long, matted hair flowing behind it. Its eyes glowed red against its deathly pale skin, sunken and hollow.

And then it was gone.

Hisako's eyes darted around the room, searching as best she could while tied to the bed. She lay back down, staring at the ceiling above, her eyes heavy, and her mind exhausted from the sedative.

The side of the mattress sank under the weight of mangled hands; amused giggles reverberated in Hisako's ear. Hisako held her breath as red eyes peered at her from the edge of the bed.

# Did You Hear That?

Saitama, Japan 2020

"I WONDER HOW much longer Sergeant Sasaki's going to be…" Kawada wondered aloud, glancing at his watch and tapping his foot. "He's been gone for over an hour."

"Less talk, more walk," Officer Honda replied irritably, dabbing his drenched forehead with his handkerchief.

Warm light poured through the windows on the second floor of Ōmiya Station as the sun sank beneath the horizon. The number of people passing through the station had decreased significantly, making their jobs much easier.

Kawada looked at his watch again.

*Twenty more minutes before we can clock out for the day. Although I doubt Sergeant Sasaki would approve of us leaving before he gets back. Hmm?*

A little girl by the escalator caught his eye. She only looked around five years old, and the surrounding adults were walking straight past her.

Kawada nudged Officer Honda's arm, whistling, then pointing to her. Officer Honda trailed behind Kawada as they walked over to talk to her, but she darted down the escalator before either of them could say a word.

"Damn. Come on, that leads down to the subway. There aren't any barriers up yet, so it could be dangerous." Officer Honda nodded in agreement and followed Kawada.

"God, it's even hotter down here…" Kawada groaned, fanning himself with his gloved hand. It didn't help much. The heat only intensified the musty smell and made the air thick and stifling.

"It's dangerous down here. Come on out. We're here to help you," Officer Honda called out softly, his voice echoing through the tunnels. There were only a few people waiting for the train. The rest were drunk or homeless people sleeping on the platform.

"Excuse me, did you see a little girl pass through here?" Kawada asked, but they all shook their heads, if they responded at all. The xylophone scale played over the loudspeaker, announcing the next train.

まもなく、川越線に駒川方面行きがまいります。

*The train bound for Kamagawa on the Kawagoe Line will arrive*

*momentarily.*

危ないですから黄色い線までお下がりください。

*Please wait behind the yellow line.*

The train sped past, stopping only briefly to collect its few passengers before disappearing back down the tunnel.

It made one hell of a racket.

Kawada and Honda scoured every corner of the platform for the girl, but she'd vanished. "She probably just went back up the escalator," Officer Honda said peevishly. "Let's go see if Sergeant Sasaki's back."

"No way. We followed her straight down. We would've seen her if she'd gone back up." Kawada removed the flashlight from his belt and shone it down the left tunnel. "That's the only place we haven't checked yet."

"In the tunnel? On the tracks? Are you insane?"

"We have to at least rule it out. There's ten minutes before the next train arrives. It'll be fine," Kawada said. He looked both ways before jumping from the platform onto the tracks. He shone the light down the left tunnel, watching where he stepped. The last thing he wanted was to brush against the high-voltage third rail in the middle of the tracks. *That would be a shitty end to a shitty day...*

He looked back at Honda, still standing on the platform. "You coming, or what?"

The lights in the tunnel were as constant as strobe lights at a rave. Kawada felt like he was on the set of a horror movie. The sound of footsteps behind him made his heart skip a beat. His flashlight flickered before fading completely, leaving him in the dark. "Goddamn it..." He gave it a few hard whacks with his hand, bringing it back to life for two brief flashes before it went out entirely.

The footsteps behind him got louder.

He braced himself, taking on the fighting stance taught in the martial arts classes at the police academy, when a bright light shone in his face. "Need a light?" Honda asked, smirking as he held up his flashlight.

Kawada exhaled, not realising he had been holding his breath. "Glad you could make it. Now let's hurry so we can get out of here."

Officer Honda flicked the light from one side of the tunnel to the other as they searched for any sign of the girl.

"Did you hear that?" he asked.

Kawada stopped a moment, barely breathing as he listened. Only the buzzing of flickering lights and air passing through the tunnel.

"You're imagining things." Kawada walked on ahead of Officer Honda. "Shine the light over here a second."

Officer Honda took one step before freezing. "There it is again. I knew I heard something." He spun around, taking the light with him and scanning the area behind him.

"We don't have time for this—" Kawada began, but was cut off. SCRIIIIIIIITCH

SCRAAAAAAAATCH

Kawada's heart stopped. "Heard it that time."

SCRIIIITCH

SCRAAAATCH

It was getting louder. And faster.

SCRIIITCH    SCRAATCH

SCRITCH    SCRATCH

Everything went dark as the flashlight fell to the ground and Officer Honda's screams echoed throughout the tunnel. There was a growl, like a dog, followed by the scraping sounds of something heavy being dragged along the ground, then a spine-chilling crunch. Kawada's ragged breathing sounded as loud as a helicopter in the subsequent silence, his heart pounding so fast he thought it would explode.

He fumbled along the floor in the darkness for Officer Honda's flashlight. Something warm and wet covered the ground, making his palms slick.

"Honda?" he whispered before finally touching the cool metal of the flashlight. After almost dropping it several times, catching it like a slippery fish, he finally got his grip on it. He felt for the rubbery soft push button on the side and clicked it in. The tunnel was bathed in red light.

Thick, dark blood covered Kawada's hands and knees where he had crawled along the floor. Crimson drag marks stretched halfway down the tunnel, well out of sight.

"What… the hell…?"

Officer Honda lay further up the tunnel in a pool of blood that spread from one side of the passage to the other; his spine and organs hanging out of the gaping hole in his torso. Arms outstretched towards Kawada, Officer Honda's eyes and mouth were wide open, screaming.

Kawada tried to choke out a scream, but nothing came out. The blood-stained flashlight clanged when it fell to the ground, sliding out of Kawada's trembling hands.

Officer Honda's lower body was gone. All that remained were the drag marks leading from his body down the tunnel. Kawada slowly backed away, his breath rapid as he reached for the flashlight. He felt cold, and the stench of blood made him sick.

Then he remembered the radio strapped to his hip.

He whipped it out of the holster; the radio making a whirring sound when he clicked the button to make contact.

"Sergeant Sasaki, Sergeant Sasaki! Requesting reinforcements in the Kawagoe tunnel. We have a man down. There's something down here. Hur—"

SCRIIIIIIIIITCH

SCRAAAAAAAATCH

His thumb slid off the receiver button. With the sound reverberating through the tunnel, it could've been coming from anywhere. It was all around him.

Sergeant Sasaki's static voice cut through the radio as Kawada scanned the tunnel for the source of the dragging sound. "Kawada? Can you repeat that? Kawada?"

SCRIIITCH

SCRAAATCH

It was getting closer again. Then it stopped.

Kawada felt warm breath on the nape of his neck and

heavy breathing in his ear. He looked as far back as he could without turning his head, relying on his peripheral vision.

Glowing eyes peered at him; the creature grazed its long, needle-like claws up his arm and along his chest. Its delighted giggles sounded almost human as it grazed his

skin with each deadly digit.

"Kawada? Come in, Kawada?" Sasaki said, only just getting off the train back to Ōmiya Station after seeing the little girl safely home. He held the radio up to his ear, listening carefully for a reply. A loud grating noise broke through the static:

SCRIIIITCH

Then a pause.

SCRAAAATCH

The sound transported him back ten years to the Urawa Police Station and the image he had tried to forget on the security footage. His heart skipped a beat. For a moment, he thought it had stopped entirely. He took flight, darting through the crowd of commuters, leaping over the ticket wicket and sprinting to the Kawagoe Line platform.

"Hang tight, I'm almost there! Kawada?"

Still no reply. Sasaki changed the radio frequency to the Ōmiya Police Station. "This is Sasaki, requesting immediate backup at Ōmiya Station in the Kawagoe tunnel. We have an officer down, maybe two. I'm en route now. Hurry!"

"Roger, Sasaki. Reinforcements are on the way."

The reply came through without a trace of static.

Sasaki tried Kawada again, with no luck. Only static, followed by the sound of something being dragged.

He sped down the escalator to the Kawagoe platform, flashlight in hand, shining it down each of the tunnels. The platform was deserted. If anyone had seen which tunnel Kawada and Honda had gone down, they were long gone.

*Fuck!* Sasaki shone his flashlight left, then right. His heart pounded in his ears, deafening him. *What the fuck were they doing down here in the first place? I told them t—*

SCRIIIIIIITCH

SCRATCH

It was coming from the left tunnel.

Sasaki took a deep breath, exhaling slowly. He climbed down the ladder onto the tracks, tiptoeing along the edge, away from the lethal third rail as he made his way to the entrance of the tunnel.

The air was stale, rank, and downright disgusting. Sasaki resisted the urge to cover his nose with his pocket handkerchief and pressed on down the tunnel, his flashlight the only source of light.

"Kawada? Honda?" he shouted, his voice bouncing off the walls throughout the tunnel. He waited for a reply—a shout, a groan, a cry—anything that might lead him to his subordinates. Instead, he got an unexpected reply; the screaming of a child, followed by another.

And another.

And another, until a chorus of children's cries filled the tunnels. Sasaki's fingertips tingled, numb from the sudden intense cold. His body felt like lead.

He hadn't had nightmares in years, but it all came flooding back. The mutilated corpses—so heart-breakingly small—clawing at him and dragging him down until he was drowning in the mass of rotting flesh.

SCRITCH

SCRATCH

The sound snapped Sasaki from his waking nightmare, making him drop his flashlight. He could hear it rolling across the tunnel floor with a clang when it hit something—one of the tracks, or the tunnel wall, perhaps.

He could almost dance to his heartbeat; his ragged breathing suddenly seemed dangerously loud. An angular stream of cool light shone from across the tunnel where his flashlight now lay.

SCRIIITCH

SCRAAATCH

*That was definitely louder...* Sasaki thought, trying to steady his breathing.

He took a tentative step forward, carefully watching where he stepped to minimise the sound of his footsteps. They were so loud, amplified by the darkness.

*Almost got it,* Sasaki thought, his arm outstretched. His fingertips brushed the cool metal, just out of reach. *Dammit...*

Sasaki took a reluctant step forward, painfully aware of the terrifying array of sounds resonating throughout the tunnel.

SCRIIIIITCH          SCRAAAATCH.

A chorus of children's screams. A low growl, the yawl of a frightened cat.

SCRIIIIITCH          SCRAAAATCH

The popping of cartilage, tearing of sinew, and crunching of bone. Sasaki didn't want to stick around long enough to find out the source of the sounds.

He picked up his flashlight, his thumb hovering over the 'on' button, and backed away slowly. *Slow and steady*, he thought, trying not to lose his footing in the dark.

*Where are those fucking reinforcements?* It felt as if he'd been down there for hours. But according to the glow-in-the-dark hands on his wristwatch, it had only been five minutes. Sasaki felt his ankle hit one of the tracks. He cried out as he tried to keep his balance. His stomach dropped as his shout rang throughout the tunnel, as if on a loop.

*If she didn't know I was here before, she certainly does now.*

Sasaki kept his thumb poised over the 'on' button of his flashlight, taking on a fighting stance, ready to run. He wiped the sweat stinging his eyes and waited for what felt like an eternity.

SCRIIITCH                              SCRAAATCH

SCRIITCH            SCRAATCH            SCRITCH

SCRATCH  SCRITCH  SCRATCH  SCRITCH

SCRATCH SCRITCH SCRATCH SCRATCH SCRITCH SCRATCHSCRITCHSCRATCH-SCRITCHSCRATCH

Sasaki punched in the button on his flashlight just long enough to light in front of him for a split second. The creature lunged at him; its clawed hands extended. He screamed and dropped his flashlight, plunging the tunnel back into darkness. Sharp claws pierced his legs.

Sasaki's screams echoed through the tunnels, growing quieter and quieter; his fingernails splitting as he clawed the ground.

SCRITCH SCRATCH

SCRITCH
SCRATCH

SEEING IS
BELIEVING

# Acknowledgements

There are so many wonderful people who have helped me on my four to five-year writer's journey thus far.

My parents and friends have always been so supportive of my endeavours. Their encouragement, reassurance, and support are what made it possible for me to do what I love.

After reading this very novella, my mum asked me, "…Should I be worried about you?"

To which I replied, "No, but thank you."

Such a tremendous compliment—thanks, Mamma. Just the confidence boost I'd needed.

My mentor, Ronnie Smart, has been the biggest contributor to my development as a writer. He took the first draft of this book (which makes me cringe, looking back—the writing itself was the definition of rough) and gave me honest but kind feedback; all of which I still use to this day. Thank you, Ronnie, for putting so much of your limited time into helping an aspiring young writer in this amazing genre. Thank you to all at the Hagley Writers' Institute, firstly for having such a brilliant course in writing, but also for helping form the connections between aspiring New Zealand writers; welcoming us into the writing community, which is such a wonderful place to be. And for not being put off by my exceedingly dark stories, having been the only horror writer in attendance.

And, of course, a big heartfelt thanks goes to my first two beta readers, Brendan and Frankie, who never failed to read my work, give me honest feedback (and have a collective giggle over my horrendous typos) and backed me all the way, through every little step. I cannot overstate how influential you both have been and how much your support at such an early stage gave me the confidence to actually pursue my goals to become a published author.

Huge thanks to my beta reader (and editor), Sharron McKenzie; and a special thanks to David Stone, who not only beta read my story, but helped me produce the audiobook with his expert advice and equipment.

# Afterword

When I first started writing, I was immensely fascinated by Japanese urban legends. I can safely say that researching these are what got me into horror in the first place.

I used to be the one who would close my eyes during horror movie trailers, shouting, "la la la la—I'm not listening, I can't hear this!" because I freely admit it: I scared very easily. It was only later, once my eyes had been opened by these delectably creepy legends, that I realised the reason for this: At night, alone in the dark, my mind was digesting and regurgitating the ghosts, ghouls, and horrific scenes I had seen, and was amplifying them.

Which scared me shitless.

*The Legend of Teketeke* was one of the first fully formed horror stories I felt compelled to write. Why, you may ask? Whilst reading up on these legends, the vengeful spirits seemed so cruel and evil and I found myself wondering...why? They're all spirits, which means they were all once human. What could have happened—what kind of death—could be so horrific that it could twist these (presumably) once good people into such terrifying, homicidal monsters? That's when I decided to write this collection. But then I thought: What if one of these creatures hadn't been a good person in life?

The only legend I seemed to have difficulty with conjuring a redemption arc for was Teketeke. So, I took that question and built on it. And what I found is that for many people, the scariest thing imaginable is not the supernatural. Not the things that go bump in the night. Not any ghost or creature of the dark. No.

The scariest monster on the face of the planet is the one that stares back in the mirror. A human can appear to be harmless—maybe even kind or charming, like Ted Bundy—when they are, in fact, quite the opposite.

When I shared the first draft of this with my first beta reader (an amazing co-worker, horror enthusiast, and a mother) she told me that what sent chills down her spine was the idea that this could actually happen. And does, unfortunately, happen. All too often.

And that is any parent's worst nightmare.

So here I am—the former scaredy-cat who had to sit at the back of the class when we dissected a cow's eyeball in high school science—living and breathing horror and loving every second of it; hoping to, in the best way possible, scare you all shitless.

I would also like to note, that Japan is actually a very safe country. They work incredibly hard to cultivate and maintain a safe society where their children can grow with a certain degree of independence from a young age; which is to be commended.

Unfortunately, every country in the world (including Japan) has monsters like Sayoko, whose sole purpose in life is to do harm to others.

# About the Author

E. L. Julian is a horror and historical fiction writer with a bachelor's degree in Japanese.

Having lived and attended a university in Nagoya, Japanese language and culture are a huge part of her identity as an artist and writer.

Originally an aspiring manga artist, E. L. Julian found solace and catharsis in writing (horror especially) after being diagnosed with rheumatoid arthritis and a string of other chronic conditions.

Her short horror stories and pieces of micro-fiction, *Wolves in Sheep's Clothing*, *Space Invaders*; *Helping Hands*, *Moonlit Monsters*, and *Symphony of Screams* have been published in the 'Cryptids and Conspiracies' and '100 Ways to Die' anthologies by Crow's Feet Journal.

Born and raised in Christchurch, New Zealand, she

enjoys watching Korean dramas and horror movies, reading manga, and making custom dolls for her YouTube channel, Kreepy Kitty Creations, many of which are recreations of characters from her books.

**Website**: eljulian.com

**Facebook**: E. L. Julian - Horror Writing Introvert

**Instagram**: @e.l.julian

**YouTube:** E. L. Julian-Horror-Writing Introvert

Kreepy Kitty Creations

# THIRSTY FOR MORE BLOOD?

Subscribe to E. L. Julian's newsletter!

Be the first to know when a new book comes out, see book cover reveals early, and get exclusive content & giveaways.

Not to mention a free eBook sneak peek into one of the next novellas from the *Seeing is Believing* collection:

**Mary's Calling**

(*Mary-san no Denwa*)

www.ingramcontent.com/pod-product-compliance
Lightning Source LLC
Chambersburg PA
CBHW032032050726
47590CB00006B/2380